Praise for *The*

'In this darkly deli...
Mas explores grief, tra...
the walls of Paris's infamous Salpêtrière hospital'
**Paula Hawkins, author of *The Blue Hour*
and *The Girl on the Train***

'A beautifully written debut set in Paris in 1885,
Victoria Mas's characters come to life within a sentence
while her storytelling compels you to turn the page'
AJ Pearce, author of *Dear Mrs Bird*

'[Victoria Mas's] portrait of women who were
unfairly banished to asylums often because they did
not fit into the straightjacket of nineteenth-century
society is moving . . . beautifully drawn'
The Times

'Elegantly written, Victoria Mas's slender, potent debut
celebrates sisterhood, while also exposing the corrupt powers
of the patriarchy at home and in the wider world'
Daily Mail

'Enthralling and wonderfully imagined . . .
written with terrific verve'
Literary Review

'Essential reading'
Cosmopolitan

www.penguin.co.uk

Also by Victoria Mas

The Mad Women's Ball

The Island of Mists and Miracles

Victoria Mas

Translated from the French by Frank Wynne

PENGUIN BOOKS

TRANSWORLD PUBLISHERS
Penguin Random House, One Embassy Gardens,
8 Viaduct Gardens, London sw11 7bw
www.penguin.co.uk

Transworld is part of the Penguin Random House group of companies
whose addresses can be found at global.penguinrandomhouse.com

First published in Great Britain in 2024 by Doubleday
an imprint of Transworld Publishers
Penguin paperback edition published 2025

Copyright © Éditions Albin Michel – Paris 2022
English translation copyright © Frank Wynne 2024

Victoria Mas has asserted her right under the Copyright,
Designs and Patents Act 1988 to be identified as the author of this work.

This book is a work of fiction and, except in the case of historical fact,
any resemblance to actual persons, living or dead, is purely coincidental.

Every effort has been made to obtain the necessary permissions with
reference to copyright material, both illustrative and quoted. We apologize
for any omissions in this respect and will be pleased to make the
appropriate acknowledgements in any future edition.

A CIP catalogue record for this book is available from the British Library.

ISBN
9781804991725

Typeset in 11.88/15.92pt Minion Pro by Jouve (UK), Milton Keynes.
Printed and bound in Great Britain by Clays Ltd, Elcograf S.p.A.

The authorized representative in the EEA is Penguin Random House Ireland,
Morrison Chambers, 32 Nassau Street, Dublin D02 YH68.

No part of this book may be used or reproduced in any manner for the purpose
of training artificial intelligence technologies or systems. In accordance
with Article 4(3) of the DSM Directive 2019/790, Penguin Random House expressly
reserves this work from the text and data mining exception.

Penguin Random House is committed to a sustainable future
for our business, our readers and our planet. This book is made
from Forest Stewardship Council® certified paper.

She told me nothing, yet I understood everything.
Alphonse Ratisbonne

All things are filled with day, even the night.
Victor Hugo

18 July 1830

The convent is silent. No rustling habit stirs the hallways. The nuns in their cornettes have forsaken the cloisters and the galleries. As they do every evening after Compline, the Daughters of Charity have retreated to their dormitory without a word; for silence, too, is prayer. The windows are open. The air is still warm. Out in the gardens, an owl stirs on its lofty branch and looks about for rodents. A distant echo of hooves serves as a reminder that the town is just outside the convent walls; landaus clatter along the Rue du Bac, drawn by horses that trot past the Mother House. Not a breath of wind cools the July night. Suddenly, from deep within the convent, there comes a clamour as the steeple bell tolls eleven o'clock. The chapel bell marks the rhythm of a time that does not belong solely to the profane. The sombre note echoes through the dormitory, hangs in the air, yet does not make the beds stir: the bodies lying beneath the sheets sleep on. Nothing will wake them. The order teaches the sisters not to allow themselves to be distracted by worldly things.

'Sister Labouré!'

Catherine, a young novitiate, opens her eyes and peers out through the white curtains that surround her bed. There is no one. She listens intently to the hushed dormitory. A few faint coughs. The drone of regular breathing. No one called out her name; she has mistaken her dream for wakefulness. She pulls the sheet around her shoulders and closes her eyes once more. Ever since she entered the Convent of the Daughters of Charity, she has had no trouble falling asleep, drifting off with the serenity of those embarking on their apostolic life.

'Sister Labouré!'

She sits bolt upright, holds her breath. This time she knows she heard a voice call out her name. Soundlessly, she leans forward to part the drapes that curtain off her bed. Her hand freezes in mid-air. A young boy is standing there, calmly staring at her, as though this is normal, as though his presence here in the sisters' dormitory at this late hour is unremarkable. The motionless novice studies the boy waiting by the foot of her bed; this child is Light.

'Sister Labouré, come to the chapel; the Blessed Virgin is waiting for you.'

All around, the bedsheets are still and silent; she alone has been woken by this boy. Without questioning the child's words, Sister Catherine glances towards the door: the old wood creaks the moment it is pushed, a disagreeable sound that hinders all attempts at discretion. It would be unwise for her to leave the dormitory; she would surely wake the others. Hearing her thoughts, the boy smiles.

'Have no fear, they are all asleep. Come.'

Then, without waiting, he turns on his heel and walks away. Sister Catherine jumps out of bed, hurriedly pulls on her habit; not for a moment does she yield to doubt, since there is no merit in doubting the miraculous. She puts her wimple over her hair and slips out of the dormitory.

Outside, the night seems startlingly bright. Every star that spangles the cloudless sky is as visible as it would be in the heart of the countryside, the waning moon silvering the rooftops of Paris. The blue glow that streams through the windows disperses the shadows of the hallway. Without pausing to marvel at the night, Sister Catherine moves through the convent, her footsteps feverish. The slightest sound causes her to catch her breath and peer into the gloom; at any moment, she might be surprised by the nuns who take over the watch at midnight. On her left, the boy walks on serenely, knowing they will encounter no one, confident that his halo will ward off all things contrary to his will. His whole body, from his curly locks to his bare feet, is enveloped in a soft glow, and Sister Catherine refrains from wondering about its source. Truth be told, she does not question anything: this is the surest way to remain calm.

At the foot of the stairs, the chapel is closed. Without slowing his gait, the boy touches the door with one finger, and it opens. When she reaches the threshold, the young novice stops, frozen; the tiny chapel is illuminated by hundreds of candles. A vigil. She has forgotten. She will have missed the opening liturgy, and her tardy arrival will disturb the silent prayer. Such carelessness will surely warrant a sanction from the Mother Superior. She glances around the nave, looking for novitiates at prayer. But the pews are empty. The altar is deserted. From the doorway to the chancel, the chapel flickers with countless flames, but there is not a living soul within. Sister Catherine sees that the boy is standing next to the sanctuary, waiting for her. She moves to join him. The floorboards creak beneath her feet. The chapel is spartan, devoid of all embellishment; only the sisters of the Mother House worship here.

Tonight, as she steps into the chantry, she once again remembers the dream that first called her to the faith some years ago, when she was still a laywoman: on that night, a face appeared to her, the face of an old man wearing a black skullcap, a white collar highlighting his wrinkled face, his warm and selfless smile. 'One day, you will be happy to come to me. Almighty God has great plans for you.' Shortly afterwards, she happened upon a portrait of Saint Vincent de Paul and recognized the face, the black skullcap, those eyes devoid of pride or scorn: the priest of whom she had dreamed was the founder of the Company of the Daughters of Charity. Dreams were never anything other than encounters.

As she reaches the foot of the altar, Sister Catherine looks around and, seeing the child, hopes that he will say something – yet like the statues, he utters not a word but simply contemplates the empty nave. Not knowing what to do, Sister Catherine kneels before the altar. She listens. The groan of the ancient wooden balconies. The crackle of an altar candle as it slowly gutters out. The whisper of a draught beneath the door. Suddenly, the bell tolls, a rumbling that fills the chapel like a thunderclap. Twelve peals announcing midnight. The last echo fades, and once again the night is silent. The novice counts the minutes. Her eyelids droop only to flick open again. Her body wavers, tips forward, rights itself in a struggle against weariness that seems lost before it has begun. Her eyelids close once more. She is about to yield to the night when, close by, she hears the boy whisper:

'The Blessed Virgin is at hand.'

Sister Catherine feels herself stiffen. Her clasped hands fly to her chest. Her breath is suspended. From behind her, a swishing sound. A mantle. Unmistakably the rustle of fabric drawing nearer. Sister Catherine presses her hands more tightly to her bosom; she can feel a presence next to her: here, on the altar steps, a silken flash of a white unlike any she has ever seen, whiter than a snow-shrouded winter landscape or the marble interior of some fine lady's dressing room, a white that seems incongruous here on earth – and this immaculate silk is covered by a mantle of blue, yet this is not the blue of sea or sky, but an azure that summons another world, something that she has been striving towards ever since she postulated with the Daughters of Charity.

Having ascended the altar steps, the figure sits upon a velvet chair.

'Behold the Blessed Virgin.'

The child's voice provokes no reaction. Surely, the Queen of Heaven could not arrive in such a simple fashion, as if she were just one of the nuns from the convent, sitting down on this dusty, threadbare chair amid the tremulous glow of candles. Sister Catherine studies the stranger's face, vainly searching for some feature, some sign by which she might recognize the figure to whom she has prayed since her childhood. Her bewilderment seems to vex the child, who takes a step closer to the chancel and, in a voice that is no longer a boy's but the grave, commanding tone of a man, proclaims:

'Behold the Blessed Virgin.'

The booming echo shakes the novice. Suddenly, as though until this moment she has been blinkered by her own fear, she sees. The face beneath the diaphanous veil. The halo that adorns the figure. The grace of her mere presence. She feels herself being thrust forward. Her legs, no longer numb with tiredness, propel her to the place where the noble figure sits enthroned. She feels her pulse pounding in her temples. Instinctively, she lays her hands on the hallowed knees, rests against this act of grace that has been granted her. She looks up into the smiling face bent over her.

She recognizes the vision now. The faithful always recognize her.

I
A HOLY SISTER

The present day

Gulls wheeled high above the old port. It was the last ferry of the day: already the skies over Roscoff had begun to grow dark. Winter was quick to sound the hour and summon people home. A traveller walked slowly along the quay towards the main road. The curve of a backpack above the shoulders, a hat shielding the face from the wind. The figure walked on, hands gripping the straps of the bag, past groups of children larking on the sand, peering into rock pools and pointing at the crabs' legs and oyster shells left by the tide. Their grandparents had warned them, had reminded them that Man could not fall where he was born, for though the sea had once been his cradle, his home was now on dry land.

The traveller walked across to the bus stop, set

the rucksack down next to the empty bench, arched his back and stretched, oblivious to the sound of approaching footsteps.

'Do you have a light?'

The traveller turned. In front of him was a little woman of advancing years, wearing the blue habit of the Daughters of Charity. She raised her cigarette and, intuiting what he was thinking, she said:

'Even we nuns have our vices.'

The traveller rummaged in his pockets and took out a lighter. Gripping her wimple to avoid it being whipped around by the wind, Sister Delphine lit her Gauloise, thanked the man, then walked over and leaned against the harbour wall. Above her, the scudding clouds were tinged a blazing pink that proclaimed the bitter cold of late winter. From her coat, Sister Delphine took a sheet of paper which she unfolded:

Delphine, my dear Sister in Christ,

I hope that by the time you receive this letter, your grief will have abated somewhat. All of us here at the Mother House are still mourning Sister Bernadette. In calling her to Himself, the Almighty must have felt that her mission here on earth was complete. It is this thought that consoles us.

> *I am pleased to inform you that soon you will have company in your lonely mission. One of our most devout sisters is going to join you on the first day of the winter holiday. Sister Anne Alice has been with us at the Mother House for more than twenty years, but her story goes back further still: at the tender age of thirteen, she came to our chapel to pray to the Blessed Virgin. In a way, this house has always been her home. I should perhaps point out that Sister Anne Alice has never ventured beyond the convent on the Rue du Bac, so this mission will be her first. It was she who insisted on going to work alongside you in Roscoff. Perhaps the call of the sea prevailed over humdrum city life! I feel she will be a great asset to our community and your mission.*
>
> *I entrust her to your care, and I remember you both in my prayers.*
> *Sister Françoise*

In the distance, the headlights of an approaching bus shimmered on the wet road. It pulled up at the stop, the doors opened, and the first passengers alighted. Among them was a woman wearing a blue wimple. Sister Delphine tucked the letter back into her pocket and folded her hands in her lap.

'Hear my prayer, oh Lord, please let her not be a prude or a prig.'

Tossing her cigarette butt to the ground, Sister Delphine straightened up and waved. The other nun eventually noticed her and, picking up her suitcase, left the gaggle of travellers. She did not seem unduly tired after the long journey from Paris: she walked briskly, keeping her eyes on the road, and had no trouble carrying her luggage. She was one of those figures people would notice, though she did not seek attention, still less seem to enjoy it.

'Hello, I'm Sister Anne.'

She took Sister Delphine's hand in hers. It was a warm, affectionate gesture. A few crow's feet lined the corners of pale green eyes that were gentle yet perceptive, inspiring trust and affection. Her veil neatly framed her perfectly proportioned features, but for an unruly lock of chestnut hair that fell across her forehead. Looking at her, one scarcely noticed the dark blue material that symbolized her faith, the white collar that signified a life of self-abnegation, the formless shift that marked her out as one committed to the service of the poor: Sister Anne wore her habit as if it were a second skin.

'I was much saddened to hear about Sister Bernadette.'

Few things saddened Sister Delphine less than her recent bereavement, the dearly departed having been the most sanctimonious madam she had had to put up with for the past two years. She casually crushed the smouldering cigarette with her shoe.

'Oh, I have shed many a tear. Shall we go?'

She turned on her heel and headed towards the historic centre of the town. The dark granite facades of the buildings were dotted with strange figures: an angel carved above a wooden door; a saint perched on the corner of an alleyway; gargoyles, shipwrights and dragons peering down from the rooftops of this ancient port where pirates and corsairs had once plied their trade, a city frozen in time for five hundred years that only seemed to rouse itself now that night was drawing in.

As they came to the crossroads, Sister Delphine pointed to a squat ancient building with a small clock tower.

'That's the old chapel dedicated to Saint Anne. You'll see her name everywhere here. Bretons are very attached to their patron saint.'

Glancing over her shoulder, Sister Delphine saw that no one was following her. She was completely alone.

Sister Anne had walked across to the quay and was gazing out at the ancient harbour, her suitcase at her feet. Her eyes scanned the jetty, searching among the moored boats for the vision Sister Rose had foretold a fortnight earlier. One morning, shortly after Lauds, as the other Daughters of Charity were silently making their way to the refectory, Sister Anne was lagging behind, still lulled by the dawn prayers, when a gnarled hand gripped her arm: 'It came to me in a dream last night – you'll witness an apparition of the Blessed Virgin in Brittany.' Turning, she had seen Sister Rose smiling at her, as she always did when night presented her with intimations of the future; as she always did when time proved her predictions to be correct. In her hoarse, gravelly voice, she whispered: 'I saw it as clearly as I see you standing here.' When they reached the refectory, the two women fell silent and did not speak of the matter again. Three days passed. Then news of a death in one of the provincial communities had reached the convent: Sister Bernadette had been called to God, leaving only one holy sister, who could not cope alone. A volunteer was urgently needed. The community in question was in Brittany, at the northern tip of Finistère.

'Sister Anne.'

Looking round, she saw Sister Delphine – teeth chattering and visibly annoyed – beckoning her to follow, so she headed back along the quay. Great looming clouds, coal-black and threatening a storm, now blanketed the harbour and the granite city. *It came to me in a dream last night – you'll witness an apparition of the Blessed Virgin in Brittany.* Clutching her suitcase, Sister Anne glanced back at the harbour one last time, as though the promised vision might appear at any moment. *I saw it as clearly as I see you standing here.* A soft roar cleaved the darkness; a pleasure cruiser coming in to moor alongside the jetty. Dozens of white shapes bobbed and dipped in the harbour, a ballet of ghosts upon the dark waters. The cruiser cut its engine and became one more phantom among a host of others. Night called all things back to land, and all respected its law.

Reluctant to keep the other nun waiting, Sister Anne hurried back up the quay under the glow of the streetlamps.

'Do you have any plans for the holidays?'

His mother plunged a plate into the sink and scrubbed at it with a dish sponge. Next to her, drying the glass she had just handed him, Hugo gave an amused smile.

'I haven't signed up to a gym, if that's what you're wondering.'

'It would do you good to take a little physical exercise. There's the football club in Saint-Pol-de-Léon. Or you could play basketball.'

She took the plate from the water, rinsed it under the hot tap. Plumes of steam rose, leaving a mist of condensation on the tiles; outside the window, the winding island paths merged in the darkness.

'Well, if you don't want to go running around after a leather ball, why not take up a martial art? Judo, maybe? That's something you might enjoy.'

Glancing over her shoulder, she was unsurprised to see her son's sardonic smile. Dimples creased his chubby cheeks. The dark peach fuzz that shadowed his upper lip did little to change his boyish features. Some days earlier, Hugo had turned sixteen; he seemed to be coasting through his adolescence, without any need to challenge authority – or resort to the cliché of teenage rebellion – to find his identity. Some rebels found their cause in books.

'Any sport, it doesn't matter. It would make your father happy.'

The phone ringing in the next room startled her: she was not expecting a call for at least two days. Hurriedly, she turned off the taps, handed the wet plate to her son, and struggled to remove the rubber gloves as she heard her husband calling out from the living room:

'It's Mathias on the phone!'

'Coming.'

Hugo dried the plate, indifferent to the flurry of excitement created by these phone calls: since leaving home, his elder brother had managed to turn his absence into a virtue.

His mother tossed the gloves into the sink.

'Can you finish up without me?'

Hugo nodded tolerantly. His mother stepped over and ran her fingers through the thick dark hair that was so like her own.

'Just make an effort, Hugo. It might bring the two of you closer.'

She turned and left the kitchen. The room was silent. Hugo opened the cupboard door and stacked the plate on top of the others. He had sometimes wondered whether his brother did it on purpose; whether he deliberately telephoned just after dinner so that Hugo would be forced to do the dishes by himself, a reminder that he could wind his little brother up, even from a different continent. He instantly regretted the thought; he was pitted against his brother too often by other people to want to do it himself. The window was covered with thick condensation. He reached out, wiped the glass and stared at the darkness shrouding the coast: there were no clouds now, and stars blazed in the night. A smile lit up his face and he quickly finished the washing up, gave the sink a final wipe, left the kitchen and headed up to his room, taking the stairs two at a time. He turned on his desk lamp – an illuminated globe of Mars, showing every crater on the surface. Above the desk hung posters of constellations and maps of the solar system. Taking a craft knife, Hugo knelt on the floor next to a package. He had let it sit, untouched, since his birthday, having decided only to open it when there was finally a cloudless night sky. He peeled off the Sellotape and ripped away the wrapping paper to discover a thick layer of bubble wrap protecting the result of two years of pleading with his parents.

Carefully, he picked it up: the astronomical telescope weighed less than he'd imagined. His hands moved over the instrument. He examined the mounting plate, the eyepiece, the optical tube; quickly skimmed through the user's manual. Here, on his knees on the floor, his exploration of the heavens had already begun as he focused on every detail of this apparatus that could perceive what mankind could never constrain: the universe and the myriad worlds contained within it. Glancing at his watch, Hugo quickly got to his feet and pushed the empty box next to a pile of books he had not yet had time to read. Having recently discovered the theory of parallel universes, he had ordered books on the subject by Brian Greene and Michio Kaku. He pulled on his anorak, grabbed the telescope and left the bedroom.

Out in the corridor, he slowed as he passed a closed door: no sound came from within. Julia was probably sound asleep. She had been coughing all through the previous night and had not settled until dawn; Hugo had jolted awake each time her hoarse wheezing started up, each time his parents went to take turns sitting by her bedside. Ever since she was born, his little sister had had to endure nights when it seemed she might never catch her breath. He decided against knocking on her door and headed downstairs.

In the living room, the television was on:

'... In other news, a minor earthquake measuring 4.7 on the Richter scale has been recorded off the coast of Finistère. Tremors from the quake were felt as far away as Brest and Quimper, but those living on the coast were told there is no risk of a tidal wave...'

His father was sitting on the sofa watching the end of the news, with one hand on the armrest and the other draped across the leather back. Michel Bourdieu was staring at the screen in exactly the same way that he stared at his students, with the commanding air that never left him, even at night, when he was not lecturing pupils about history. The calfskin cushions bowed under the weight of his hulking frame; the floor beneath the sofa creaked. His father's mere presence seemed to weigh on everything.

'Where's Maman?'

Without looking at his son, Michel Bourdieu picked up the remote control and changed channels. A cross hung on the wall above the sofa; Christ seemed to be leaning down to study the balding pate of the master of the house.

'She's up in her room. She was very upset by your brother's call. There's been an explosion in Mali, in Ménaka – a car bomb. Thankfully, Mathias wasn't hurt, but two of the soldiers in his regiment were killed.'

Michel Bourdieu finally turned towards the doorway and studied his younger son, who lacked both the stature and the self-assurance of his brother, and whose very presence was enough to spark a feeling of contempt that he could not control. Some children are defined by all the things they are not.

'Are you going out?'

'I'm going to try out the telescope. I'll be back in an hour.'

'It's pitch-black outside.'

'That's kind of the point?'

Michel Bourdieu grumpily turned away. From around his neck came the flash of a gold crucifix. Gritting his teeth, he switched channels again.

'Try not to fall into the sea. You can't swim, remember?'

A strident political debate filled the living room. Hugo stared at his father's implacable profile as though this man were a stranger, as though he needed to convince himself that they were indeed related. A child is never really sure that they are from their parents' blood.

A sea breeze ruffled the grass of the lawns along the coast. Closing the garden gate behind him, Hugo walked down the deserted path using his flashlight to guide him. Although he knew the island now, he had not yet learned to trust the bluish glow of cloudless nights; until this point, the only glow that had illuminated his nightly walks had come from the streetlights in Paris. He set off. The lapping of the waves accompanying his footsteps was a constant reminder of the shore below. Halfway down the path, he turned right and took a track that led up into the sand dunes. Behind him, the sea finally fell silent. It was here, amid the tall grasses, that he had first discovered true silence; a silence that he had never experienced in Paris, where every instant was troubled by some echo of the city. It was only when he'd come here, to live on the Isle of Batz off the coast of Roscoff, and had walked up into the dunes, that he had discovered this stillness. It was like a forgotten language that had existed before all others; before Tamil and Sanskrit, before the first language ever to be heard on earth.

He carried on walking. From a hollow on his left rose the ruins of an ancient chapel, a sinister structure that seemed to come straight from a child's nightmare. Hugo continued up the dunes until he reached a flat headland. The vast star-speckled sky soared above the island and the calm sea. Even with the naked eye, he could easily make out the diaphanous tracery of the gauzy threads that linked the constellations weaving a glittering chain above the bay; looking at this pattern, it was impossible not to wonder whether, when the first spider wove its silken snare, it had modelled it on this celestial web.

Hugo set his tripod on the grass, raised it to a comfortable height, adjusted the mount. The wind began to bluster, and he pulled his hood down around his face. Pointing the lens at Mars, he tightened the focus-locking screw. Everything was ready. He stepped closer, leaned over the eyepiece. He did not have time to adjust the focus before he was distracted by the sound of approaching footsteps. Turning around, he shone his flashlight into the face of the intruder, who screwed up his eyes against the blinding glare. Hugo quickly switched off the torch and brought it to his chest.

'Sorry, Isaac.'

The boy had come from the opposite direction. He carried no torch, needing nothing more than the light from the cloudless sky to find his way; the island's paths required no illumination for those born here. He spotted the tripod set up on the grass.

'Is that a telescope?'

'Not exactly. It's an astronomical telescope, or a refracting telescope ... People often confuse the two.'

'Can I have a look?'

His pale face loomed closer in the darkness, like an apparition that might haunt a dream. The fine features, the curly fringe falling over his forehead; a delicacy that was anything but fragile. He bent over the eyepiece while Hugo stood by in silence. Unsure what to do with his hands, which he noticed were trembling slightly, he put them behind his back.

'I've trained the telescope on Mars. Actually, you can see Mars with the naked eye – it's that orange dot flickering just below Aries. The reddish colour comes from iron oxide – rust, basically. All the rocks are covered with it. The colour changes as sandstorms sweep across the surface of the planet. You can spend a whole year looking at Mars and it will never look the same way twice . . . You can't get a particularly detailed view with a telescope – you won't be able to see the craters or the polar ice caps – but you can get a much closer look. When you realize that, right now, Mars is sixty million kilometres away, it's almost . . . it's almost heart-breaking.'

The breeze had fallen silent now. It could not be heard whispering through the gorse bushes, racing across the dunes, running through the grass; it seemed to have been suspended, attuned to the voice of this boy, summoned by this familiar vibration, the connection between the things of this world.

Hugo felt his cheeks flush, embarrassed that he had used those words, allowed his tongue to outrun his thoughts. The first time he had found himself in Isaac's presence, he had been unable to say anything other than his name. That day, his father had been held up by a meeting, so Hugo had taken the bus to

Saint-Pol-de-Léon, excited to be able to go home on his own. He had got off the bus at the old port of Roscoff, then walked over to the second harbour where the ferry was already waiting. No sooner had he boarded the ferry than he stopped, frozen: sitting alone on the furthest bench, staring through the porthole, was Isaac. Hugo had seen the boy a number of times since the beginning of the school year; usually on the island, walking along the white beach, or on the road where they both lived, but he also saw him every day at school, in the playground during breaktime or coming out of the canteen. And it was this face, without a hint of arrogance or malice, that Hugo missed when he left school at the end of each day.

When he'd spotted Hugo, Isaac had gestured for him to come and sit next to him, and Hugo had moved forward, unsure whether it was the boat lurching beneath him or his feet that were unsteady. He had settled himself on the wooden bench and whispered his first name, though he was unsure whether Isaac had heard him. From that moment, he was utterly unaware of the boat reversing, slowly pulling away from the quay; unaware of the crossing that usually left him feeling seasick: for the first time, his attention was entirely focused on something back here on earth.

Stepping away from the telescope, Isaac flashed him a smile.

'You know, you ought to be teaching science at our school ... I should probably go now, Papa will be worried.'

Hugo watched as the figure melted into the darkness. Then, slowly, he turned back to his telescope; but he could see only the face of the boy who had just left.

'Should you need any further information about Option A (river boat licence), please don't hesitate to contact our school in Roscoff, or you can call me on 07 47 ...'

Alan stopped typing: he could hear the front door closing softly. He turned to look towards the lit corridor and listened intently. A minute passed. His son appeared, parka buttoned to the neck, carrying his shoes in one hand, hugging the wall and clearly hoping against hope not to hear his name.

'Isaac.'

The teenager froze, let out a sigh, and his shoulders sagged. Reluctantly, he retraced his steps and stood in the doorway. Sitting behind his computer, lit by the glow of the monitor, his father's haggard face spoke of a lack of sleep that went far beyond simple insomnia. Over the past few days, he had not shaved, and his jawline was covered with stubble that had the same salt-and-pepper colour as his uncombed hair. His eyebrows were still dark brown, the only feature that had been spared by the grief of mourning.

'There's some pasta left in the fridge.'

'I had dinner at Madenn's.'

There came the whistle of a soft breeze through the half-open window, filling the office with the smell of salt spray. Alan stiffened in his chair. He hesitated before saying anything more, struggling to find the right words. He knew how brittle these conversations could be, knew that at any moment his son could turn his back, walk away from a conversation that neither of them knew how to begin, let alone complete. He looked at the boy standing in the doorway, his cheeks still red with the cold, the unruly curl falling over his forehead, and that softness that had marked him out since childhood. It was a softness that, from an early age, had perplexed grown-ups, who were unsure whether to refer to Isaac as *he* or *she*, and would shower him with the praise they reserved for boys who possessed something of the gentleness of girls. As the years passed, though, age did not alter the delicacy of his features, and by adolescence people began to look at him differently; flattery gave way to insults, and Isaac encountered violence. On numerous occasions he had come home from school with a split lip or a black eye, having been the unwitting cause of a fight that spoke to the insecurities of boys his age. Every time Alan saw his injured son come through the door, he had had to choke back his rage and tend the wound without a word: having already experienced grief, Isaac was now experiencing what it meant to be different.

'Night, Papa.'

His son disappeared, and Alan listened as he went upstairs. The bedroom door closing, the thud of dropped shoes, the creak of floorboards under the bed. Then there was no more sound from the room. Mistakenly, Alan assumed his son was asleep. He had no idea of the nightly ritual that took place behind that closed door: lying on the bed holding a picture frame, Isaac gazed for a long time at the photograph it contained, struggling to ward off sleep; sometimes he would feel his eyelids droop, but he persisted, desperate to prolong his silent conversation with his mother, until the frame would slip from his hands and he would surrender to a dreamless sleep.

T*he tricycle lies at the foot of the magnolia tree, abandoned to the rain. The torrent has reduced the border filled with hyacinths to a series of muddy puddles. Her grandmother planted the flowers last autumn, but the magnolia tree has stood here since before she was born. From the window, Sister Anne stares out at the garden, which is being lashed by the downpour. She should have put the tricycle in the garage; her grandmother had explained to her that water rusts metal. She hears a noise behind her. Turning, she sees that the room is bathed in a murky half-light. The thunderstorm has prematurely turned day into night. She can barely make out the dolls lining the shelves; she has just put them away, because it is not playtime. The stuffed toy monkey on the bed listens to the clatter on the roof tiles with his one remaining ear. There are no toys scattered around. Her attention is drawn to a presence: a *figure perched on the edge of the bed with its back to her. A little girl. Instinctively, Sister Anne moves away from the window. Slowly, warily, she walks around the bed, trying not to scare the motionless child.*

The girl does not see the nun who comes to stand by her: she is staring fixedly at the closed door. She is waiting. Here and there, old wooden joists groan. A dampness cools the wallpaper. Suddenly, the house echoes with a creaking sound: footsteps on the wooden staircase. Someone is coming. A breath of wind chills Sister Anne to the marrow. She looks down at the girl: her face is a mask of terror as she stares at the door. The door. With a bound, Sister Anne is there, both hands fumbling in the darkness for a key, a bolt, a lock; anything that might prevent entry to the room. On the other side, the footsteps continue to climb the stairs – slowly, because this is part of the pleasure, the moment deferred, the ascent that precedes arrival. The footsteps are louder now, gloating at the thought that they can be heard, that they are in the room even before they cross the threshold. Inside, Sister Anne frantically rushes around, searching for a chest of drawers, a chair, anything that could be wedged against the door. Her eyes alight on the child: in the gloom, her ashen face is contorted, her mouth twisted into a scream, a strangled cry that never comes; it is the face of someone who has seen death. Only the girl's small hands still move, clutching at the hem of her skirt and pulling it over her knees, trying to cover her bare legs, to shield what these footsteps have come for. There is a creak on the landing: he is outside. Instinctively, Sister Anne leans against the door with all her weight; the handle turns, senses the resistance, perseveres, but Sister Anne does not waver. Digging her heels into the carpet, she redoubles her efforts, but the door slowly begins to open: the strength on the other side is much greater than her own. Sheer rage urges her on. She struggles, refuses to give in, even as the door continues to open, even as she sees his shoes through the crack. She turns and gives the girl a forlorn glance; then, suddenly, she is thrown backwards and left sprawling on the carpet. She looks up at the gaping doorway: he is here again.

Sister Anne woke with a jolt, sucking in deep lungfuls of air like a diver coming to the surface. She scrabbled back on the bed, huddling against the wall, tugging her nightdress over her bare legs all the way down to her ankles. She peered into the darkness. The familiar silhouette of a wardrobe. The legs of a desk. The crucifix above the door. There was no one there. The room was empty. Her heart was hammering; Sister Anne could hear it. She hugged her knees to her chest and curled into a ball. Her hair fell over her shoulders, brushing against her bare arms. She dared not get up yet.

Back at the convent, when she had the dream, she would grab a cardigan and step out of her cell, walk quietly through the corridors with only the glow of the stars to guide her, go out into the garden and wander the winding paths, trying to shake off the last of her fears, praying over and over to ward off this evil that had tracked her down. No one had ever seen her: the past came back to haunt her only when there were no witnesses.

Her feet slid out of the bed now and touched the cold floor. She took a shawl from the chair and wrapped it around her shoulders, the soft wool warming her skin. Soundlessly, she stepped over to the window and carefully opened the shutters; the smell of the sea took her by surprise, heightening her senses. Down below, streetlamps lit the deserted alley. Some cars were parked haphazardly in the nearby car park. The street was lined with privet hedges that separated it from the promenade running the length of the city walls; beyond them, she could sense the invisible sea. Darkness flooded every space. On the horizon, a beam of light skimmed the surface of the water, then instantly disappeared. A lighthouse. She peered into the darkness and eventually made out a second light, then another and another: a string of lights that traced the wide meanders of the shoreline.

It came to me in a dream last night – you'll witness

an apparition of the Blessed Virgin in Brittany. She heard Sister Rose's voice whisper in her ear, reminding her why she had come all this way, to this outpost by the sea, this town with no railway station; she who had never set foot outside the cloisters, who had never been tempted to go on mission, had been content to remain within the walls of the convent on the Rue du Bac, in the Mother House she had chosen to be her home since the tender age of thirteen. *I saw it as clearly as I see you standing here.* These words came back like a verse from a psalm, like a promise that responded to the vow she had pledged when she was still a little girl called Alice.

It had been Sister Rose who first noticed her in the immaculate chapel; an unobtrusive presence kneeling at the foot of the altar, her face upturned, gazing at the statue of Mary. One day, Sister Rose had approached the child, held out her hand to this motherless young girl who had been betrayed by her father and had come here to find in the bosom of the Virgin Mary something denied her by her parents – not simply a sense of presence, but more importantly, chastity. It was Sister Rose who had shown her the incorrupt body of Saint Catherine Labouré, which lay in the glass casket next to the altar, dressed in her habit, smiling beneath her white linen cornette, a rosary of ebony wound around hands clasped in prayer. She had recounted the story of how, one night, on these same altar steps, Sister Catherine Labouré had come face to face with the Blessed Virgin in one of those miracles that prove that every prayer, if it comes from the heart, is always heard.

In the years that followed, Sister Rose had watched as the timorous teenager took her first steps as a postulant, received the veil of the novitiate, chose her religious name – Sister Anne, in honour of the mother of the Blessed Virgin – and, three years later, made her religious profession, thereby becoming a Daughter of Charity, an earnest follower of Louise de Marillac and Catherine Labouré. She had watched as the girl blossomed beneath her veil, as her gestures became more assured and she acquired the special grace that elicited affection, as though already Sister Anne were among the blessed few to whom the Virgin had appeared.

Once more, the beam of the lighthouse pierced the darkness. Leaning against the window frame, Sister Anne watched as the light skimmed the surface of the water then disappeared again. The coastline shimmered, casting points of light into the night so that, in this boundless space, she felt as though she were contemplating a constellation.

Bells rang out. The panicked seagulls perched along the railings took to the wing as the belfry roared into life. A break in the clouds turned the granite to a pale ochre, the sun warming the damp caravels* carved into the stone. The church bells announced mass, spreading the word as far as the old harbour of Roscoff.

'Not all of you at once!'

A crowd had gathered on the forecourt: the faithful surged forward, craning their necks to catch a glimpse of the person who had aroused such curiosity. The young priest pushing his way through the throng raised his hands to temper their fervour. Father Erwann, a local boy, had only recently begun his ministry at Notre-Dame-de-Croas-Batz. At first, wary of

---

* A caravel is a type of ship.

his beardless, candid face, his tender years – he was barely thirty – the parishioners had argued that his narrow shoulders would not bear the burden of the cassock for very long. But on the very first Sunday, the new priest had won over his congregation with a sermon filled with nuance and wit; his innate sense of compassion and unaffected kindness had definitively put paid to the aspersions on his youth. Father Erwann was one of those priests with a sense of vocation that belied his age.

'Go gently, this is her first day!'

Finding herself the centre of attention, Sister Anne shook hands with everyone, greeting them with a smile, patting their shoulders as though she had lived here all her life and knew every parishioner already. She leaned forward, her luminous green eyes meeting those of each parishioner in turn, and this was all that mattered, this wordless exchange, as if she was able to intuit the unique qualities of each individual. As she made her way through the crowd, the patch of sunlight seemed to follow this graceful yet affable middle-aged nun, and everyone she encountered had the poignant sense that they had finally been seen.

'Sister Anne, I don't believe you've met Michel Bourdieu.'

Hearing the priest's words, Sister Anne turned and saw a silhouette coming towards her, a formidable figure who completely eclipsed the sun's dazzling rays as he pushed his way through the crowd; around his neck, the gold crucifix glittered in the light.

'Sister.'

A calloused hand grasped hers, crushing her slender fingers in a manner intended to test her strength and, through it, her character. Realizing this, Sister Anne withstood the iron grip without demur, making it clear that in her time she had shaken many hands, desperate hands, hands intent on testing her resolve, and she had not once capitulated. This hand would be no exception.

'Collecting donations, recruiting volunteers, organizing catechism classes . . . I sometimes wonder where Michel finds the time to sleep!'

Oblivious to the power play, the young priest stepped closer to Michel Bourdieu as he lavished praise on his good works, his virtues not only as a person of faith but also a family man. Sister Anne studied the object of this praise: the clenched, determined jawline; the eyes obscured by an anguish whose nature she could not yet guess. Still holding his gaze, she did not disguise the irony in her smile.

'It would seem that Michel Bourdieu has all the virtues of a Daughter of Charity.'

Her comment surprised the man, and she felt the coarse hand release hers. He returned her smile; his features relaxed and his expression softened, even revealing a glimpse of warmth. Michel Bourdieu's approach to those he could not intimidate was to charm them.

'Sister Anne, allow me to present my wife.'

A little way off, a woman stood waiting in the sunshine; a slight figure who seemed so fragile one could not help but wonder how she managed to carry the young girl in her arms. With a warm and tender gesture, she took the nun's hand, just as twenty years earlier, on another occasion, she had taken Michel Bourdieu's hand – on another forecourt, that of Notre-Dame-des-Victoires in Paris, when the two students were beginning their first day of voluntary work. The normal rules of seduction weren't needed for some. That first brief touch had been enough for both of them to know that they would marry here, in the very church where they had first met.

'This shy little girl is Julia. She's the reason we moved here – Paris wasn't good for her asthma. Right now, she's very tired. She had another asthma attack last night.'

The little girl had her face pressed into her mother's perfumed neck. From time to time, she turned and surreptitiously glanced at the nun, who reminded her of the holy statues she had seen in church. The child's eyes were ringed with dark circles; she seemed resigned to the threat of her body, to nights spent struggling for breath, and for sleep; to an existence marked by struggle.

'Our eldest son, Mathias, is in the army. Right now, he's in Mali. We're very proud of him.'

As he said this, the child he had not deigned to mention appeared; a dark-haired teenager, gentle like his mother. On seeing the boy, Michel Bourdieu's tone changed:

'And this is Hugo.'

A cloud cast the square in shadow. People glanced up, startled by this unexpected grey cloak; in anticipation of the rain, the crowd began to disperse. Michel Bourdieu's wife stepped forward and invited Sister Anne to visit them on the Isle of Batz; then she and her family left, walking around the low wall that encircled the church grounds. Michel took the girl from his wife's arms, hoisted her on to his shoulders. Sister Anne watched as the family walked away, falling naturally into a rhythm all of their own, and it seemed to her that nothing could shake this fervently solid household.

Drops of water fell on to the plate. Goulven glanced up and felt more droplets splashing his forehead: it was raining on the island. Muttering to himself, he pushed back his terrace chair with a crunch of gravel, picked up his plate and pushed open the door of the restaurant's dining room, letting in a whistle of cold air. Behind the counter, Madenn was chopping chives.

'Didn't I tell you it was going to rain?'

The stocky man shrugged as he shambled awkwardly between the tables; some years earlier, he had had a fall while out fishing, leaving him with a limp that meant he could no longer trawl for shellfish. He settled himself next to the window, picked up his crab tartine with both hands and took a huge mouthful. The owner set her knife on the chopping board and shook her head.

'Greedy slob.'

She took a pinch of chives and sprinkled it over the warm omelette in front of her; Madenn prepared the food with the same care and attention as she had on the very first day she had cooked for the child. She looked up suddenly and peered out at the road that ran past the restaurant; just as she did so, the parka appeared. Its hood was pulled down low, partially obscuring the face she was waiting to see. The restaurant door swung open, bringing in a new gust of wind.

'And how's my lad?'

In a single movement, Isaac pushed back his hood and shook his hair, scattering the raindrops that clung to his curly locks. The place was empty, except for Goulven, who was still sitting by the large picture window, wolfing down the rest of his crab tartine without bothering to chew. From the local radio station came a song in Breton, a woman's keening voice singing a cappella, filling the empty restaurant with a deep and mysterious sound. Today was a far cry from the buzz of lunchtimes during high season: the tables thronged with summer visitors; boisterous, shrieking children; the smell of fish, grilled or fried; breadcrumbs strewn across the floor; ice cream that melted all over the white paper tablecloths. The long winter months deterred everyone except those who lived on the island.

'Come on now, your omelette is getting cold.'

The teenager clambered on to the bar stool. Madenn

pulled her hair back into a bun, securing the shock of purple with a flowery hairclip. A wispy fringe highlighted the blue of her eyes, and a mauve waistcoat hugged her ample curves, complementing the tawny skirt that fell to her ankles. Ever since she was a teenage girl, Madenn had worn colour as if it were a philosophy.

'Did you run into your father last night?'

'Yeah, for a couple of minutes. He was working.'

'How is he getting on these days?'

'Same as he has been for the past ten years.'

Outside on the terrace, the rain was falling heavily now. Drops bounced off the table abandoned by Goulven. Not a single car passed.

Ten years. The weather had been just like this on the day the telephone rang. A few straggling customers had just left the restaurant. Madenn had been sweeping up the crumbs between the tables and straightening the chairs. When the phone rang, she had felt a tight knot in her stomach. She had raced over and picked up the receiver, unable to bear the shrill tones. At first, she had not been able to hear anything; again and again she had asked who was calling her number. Finally, she heard a man's voice, one she did not recognize immediately. It was Alan. He was calling from the hospital. An accident while they were on their way to Brest. He and his son had survived it unscathed. But then his voice trailed off, and Madenn clapped a hand over her mouth to stifle a scream. Many years before this tragedy, long before Isaac was born, the wedding reception had been held here, in this same restaurant. All the islanders had gathered – they had toasted the couple, they had danced, they had chanted the two names now linked for life, Alan and Lucie, singing the praises of the newlyweds into the early hours, wishing them a long and happy life together, celebrating the married pair who would soon be blessed with a son. Ever since, each time Madenn looked around this dining room, each time she contemplated this space in which happiness had been made flesh, she felt as if she were looking at a room full of memories.

'He looks like he hasn't had a bite to eat in three days.'

Isaac's voice brought her back to reality, and Madenn glanced at the restaurant's only customer. Bent over his table, Goulven was savouring the last of his lunch, wiping sauce from the edge of the plate with his finger, picking up stray breadcrumbs with his fingertip. Goulven had lunch here every day. Invariably he sat out on the terrace, except when he was forced inside by the rain; each day he departed without a word, always taking the same route back to the house he now rarely left. Ever since his accident at sea, the former fisherman kept boredom at bay by sticking to a strict routine.

'Would you care for a little slice of tart, Goulven?'

The man shook his head and Madenn did not insist; she draped a tea towel over her shoulder and rinsed the frying pan under the tap, keeping her eyes trained on Isaac all the while. She could tell from his complexion that he had slept well. In the weeks that followed the terrible accident, she had often found the child here: he would flee an approaching thunderstorm and take refuge under her roof; she had found him hiding behind her counter, having run away from a gang of boys who were chasing him; she would see him sitting at a table, alone in the crowded restaurant, preferring the noise and commotion to the silent emptiness of home.

At first, she had found his visits deeply troubling: the moment he walked through the door, she was reminded of the woman who had died; he haunted the restaurant as though he himself were a ghost. Madenn did not want to see him, did not want to have to look at this face that vividly reminded her of his dead mother he so closely resembled. But since she could not stop him coming, she greeted him brusquely, paid no heed to him while he was there and did not bother to say goodbye when he left. To her surprise, the child always came back the following day, as though her callousness had had no effect on him, as though nothing could upset him now.

One night, he showed up during a rainstorm, dripping from head to foot, and Madenn, moved to pity, had reluctantly heated up a piece of quiche for him. On another occasion, he had shown up clearly unwell, and she had prepared freshly squeezed orange juice, scowling a little less harshly. As the months went by, she had found herself watching out for him, staring at the road, waiting for him to come back from school, and when he did arrive, when he walked through the door, she would ignore her other customers, she would go over and look into his face and try to intuit his mood without him saying a word. On those days when he did not come, when he went straight home, Madden would pace up and down behind her counter, stacking the cups, vainly attempting to fill the void left by this child whose visits had become the one thing she looked forward to.

From outside came the roar of an engine: a Citroën 2CV appeared and drove past the restaurant. Behind the wheel, Madenn recognized Michel Bourdieu, the new history teacher at the lycée in Saint-Pol-de-Léon. He had moved to the island at the beginning of the school year, and his presence had made her shudder the first time he brought his family for lunch at the restaurant.

'I can't abide that Bourdieu. The wife is pleasant enough, though she's a bit spineless. But him, he thinks he's a preacher! As if the people of Brittany weren't sanctimonious enough already!'

Goulven, who had been silent until now, set down

his cutlery and stared pointedly at the restaurant owner. 'Is that coffee coming?'

Madenn put a coffee cup on the espresso machine. On the radio, Storlok was playing guitar and singing 'Keleier Plogoff' – 'The Battle for Plogoff' – a hymn to the fierce resistance of the Breton people during the early 1980s, when the government in Paris had tried to build a nuclear power plant at Pointe du Raz. The melancholy strains of the *gwerz** filled the restaurant, celebrating the natives of Brittany who had stood firm against the invader, the struggle for the homeland groaning under the yoke of a foreign power. The coffee machine droned in accompaniment, filling the room with the delicious aroma of roasted arabica beans.

'Don't be hanging around now, Isaac. The bakery will be closing soon.'

The teenager glanced at the clock; he had promised his father he'd bring home fresh bread. Madenn watched until he disappeared around the corner and, as always when she watched him leave, this child she knew better than if she had given birth to him herself, she closed her eyes and prayed to the Blessed Virgin to watch over him.

---

* Breton word for a ballad or a lament.

The rain had stopped now. A boundless expanse of grey cloud hung over the island. Isaac left the bakery and headed down to the little beach next to the harbour. There was no wind; the boats at their moorings seemed to be sleeping, having waited too long for a voyage that would not come. Not a breath of wind rippled the glassy surface of the sea. With two baguettes tucked under his arm, Isaac walked along the sand, circling the ghostly port. In the distance, on the far shore, it was just possible to make out the town of Roscoff and the coastline that islanders referred to as France; the Continent – a foreign land they watched from afar, relieved that they did not have to live there.

The boy headed back towards the road and on to Notre-Dame-du-Bon-Secours, the parish church that loomed over the town and the port, keeping an eye on the boats that plied the waters surrounding the island. Next to the church, the open gates of the local cemetery; a plot of land filled with tombstones and crosses, without a soul come to pray or to sweep the dead leaves from the graves. In the neighbouring garden, the rooster was silent. There was no one else on the road. Some of the houses kept their shutters closed, only opening them at the end of this season.

Near the Rhû wayside marker, a moped flashed past, rounding the site of the granite cross and continuing on its journey, the engine farting and sputtering. Once it had disappeared, Isaac could hear nothing but the sound of his own footsteps. He walked on. The houses now were sparsely scattered, and before long the town was far behind him. A broad vista opened up of open fields tumbling towards the sea where countless rocks rose from the surface, the watered silk reflected in the clouds, the violet skin of the earth itself. His mother had left this island and Isaac, in a sense, had ceased to live here too, turning away from the desolate landscape, refusing to look upon this island where nothing existed but her absence. He felt drops on his hands: it had started to rain once more. He pulled up his hood, bowed his head, and saw nothing on his walk home but the wet tarmac beneath his feet.

Sister Delphine brought the cigarette to her lips; she tried to light it once, twice, turning her back to the wind and shielding the flame with her hands. Her wimple fluttered and whipped around her shoulders, threatening to reveal her white hair; in the time she had been living here in Roscoff, she had lost three wimples to the waves. Having lit her cigarette, she turned back towards the sea, now at high tide. A nor'easter was hurling waves against the sea wall; somehow the sound of the surf pounding against the rocks felt strangely like an embrace.

'It's so overcast, you can barely see Batz.'

Next to her, Sister Anne thought she could just make out the distant coast on the horizon, the one she had seen from her bedroom window glistening in the middle of the night. Now it was shrouded in a mist that blurred every shape, even the lighthouse to the west. The phantom island reminded her of the ghostly apparitions that had appeared to corsairs on their travels.

'I never go there myself. I can't be dealing with boats.'

Sister Delphine sat on a bench and zipped her jacket all the way up; a light drizzle was falling over the promenade. The two nuns had just come back from the old people's home where they had spent the afternoon. Passing time with the old, the lonely and those less fortunate was a significant part of their work here, and so they had visited the elderly residents, consoled those whose relatives no longer came, played Monopoly with the more cognisant – attempting to help them forget, if only for a few hours, those twilight years that were more monotonous than melancholic.

During their visit, Sister Delphine had noticed the attention being paid to Sister Anne: the hopeful glances, the outstretched hands, as though these people had always been expecting her, as though they were simply putting a face to a name. Taking languid puffs on her cigarette, Sister Delphine studied the elegant figure standing by the sea wall: her gaze attentive to every wave; her measured, mysterious reserve that elicited confessions without seeking them out.

'They tell me you found the Blessed Virgin when you were thirteen, Sister Anne.'

The phrase made Sister Anne smile. As she watched, waves crashed against the shore, eroding the coal-black rocks, ebbing and flowing in a way that kept her spellbound. True, she had been thirteen; true, she had pushed open the wooden door without thinking – it was only by chance that she had found herself there. She had been wandering around near Le Bon Marché, lingering in front of shop windows, having run away once more. Ever since her father had been convicted, sentenced to life imprisonment, she had been living in an orphanage where she, like the other children, was waiting to be adopted. Two nuns had come around the corner, dressed in light, flowing, navy-blue habits. They walked easily, happily; a far cry from the notions she had held about nuns. She had watched them walk up the Rue du Bac as far as a great stone porchway, and without knowing why, without understanding what force was guiding her steps, she had decided to follow them. She had found herself in a hushed passageway, pilgrims gazing at the votive candles and statues she did not recognize – Saint Vincent de Paul, Saint Catherine Labouré – and somehow the place, rather than intimidating her, had filled her with awe. Up ahead, the sisters went through a small wooden door. On it was a brass plaque engraved with the words:

THE ISLAND OF MISTS AND MIRACLES

It was in this very chapel
in the year of our Lord, 1830,
that the Blessed Virgin Mary
Mother of God
appeared to
Sister Catherine Labouré
and gave unto the world
the Miraculous Medal.

The creak of wood had echoed around the nave. Along the pews, all heads were bowed. Hands clasped rosary beads. The transept was pristine, perfectly white, from the columns to the archivolts; the rows of pews were bathed in light, adding to a brilliance that she had never seen elsewhere. She had stepped closer, as though pushed by some unseen hand; before her, a statue rose above the chancel: the Blessed Virgin, most pure, most merciful, carved from the finest marble, wearing a crown of glittering stars, golden rays spilling from her hands. The young girl had fallen to her knees and prostrated herself before the altar, gazing up at this figure who embodied all of the things she believed she had lost.

Buffeted by a gust of wind, Sister Anne suddenly felt dizzy: ever since she had come to this coastline, her head had been spinning and her body felt curiously numb, as though the sea required a different sense of equilibrium, demanded that she set aside all familiar reference points, the bearings she had learned back in the city.

She pulled her raincoat tighter around her and turned back to the woman who was sitting on the bench, smoking.

'I would say that it is the Blessed Virgin who knows how to find us.'

With a long groan, shutters opened and clattered against the facades of the houses. On the trees, the burgeoning boughs welcomed the first rays of dawn. The sweeping bay smouldered with every shade of crimson, setting the world ablaze even before the sun appeared above the horizon. Sitting on her bed, Madenn piled her purple hair into a chignon and fixed it with a floral clip; the early light streamed through her window, bathing the room with its warm glow. She got up and set about choosing clothes from her wardrobe; hers was the morning routine of those who wake alone and set about the day in silence, without a glance to left or right. She pulled on a long-sleeved vest, the white wool jumper that had belonged to her mother, a skirt of red cotton that fell to her ankles, and her khaki raincoat, then left the bedroom. Downstairs, the lights in the restaurant were off, the chairs stacked on top of the tables, and a few glasses sat drying next to the sink. She slipped on her wellingtons, grabbed her shopping trolley and headed out.

The smell of wood fires drifted across the narrow road. She walked along the coast, past the fallow fields and the tilled farmland, amid the bitter scent of artichokes and onions, of potatoes and cauliflowers. When she came to the wayside cross at Rhû, she took the winding lane down to the port, where the boat was waiting by the pier. She surveyed the horizon, instinctively noting the colour of the morning sky – now a pale, tranquil blue – the absence of clouds and the level of the tide, reading the signs of dawn in a reflex common to those who lived along the coast. She boarded the boat, kissed Youenn and Igor good morning, and greeted the islanders who were already aboard. The engine roared into life, and the passenger boat set off on its first crossing of the day from the island to the mainland.

In Roscoff, the white tents of the local market had been set up in the car park next to the port. Madenn was among the first customers and people called out to her, chatted with her, filled her trolley with spices and salt from Guérande. They haggled amicably, allowed her to sample dried fruits and a new local honey. She added onions, garlic and shallots, bought two loaves of freshly baked bread for the price of one, and last but not least, a bunch of tulips. The sun broke through the gaps between the stalls, gilding the vivid colours of the fruit and vegetables on display and warming her cheeks. Her shopping done, Madenn set off home, dragging the shopping trolley which groaned beneath the weight of the produce she'd bought. She stopped at the harbour cafe, where she stood at the counter, chatting with the owner and commenting on the glorious weather; the waters of the harbour were flecked with rich tints of bronze, shimmering between the old fishing boats at anchor, as though winter were trying to apologize by offering this sunlight so reminiscent of summer.

Back on the island, Madenn made her way up to the local cemetery, where an elderly woman who had been born and raised on the island was moving between the headstones, sweeping away the dead leaves. Madenn took a withered bouquet of flowers from the vase and replaced it with the tulips she had just bought, setting the vase down next to the marble headstone. She chatted to her parents in silence, since the dead can read the thoughts of those still living. She said a prayer for her mother, a woman much inclined to pray, and joked with her father, a man who loved to laugh. Then she took her trolley and headed back to the restaurant.

A few customers were lunching on the terrace; Goulven, sitting at his usual table, his face red from the sun, was guzzling a galette. In the generous warming light, the diners could shrug off the February blues for the space of their lunchtime and think that, perhaps, this winter might not be so bleak after all.

'Here, take this home with you.'

Madenn set a plate covered in clingfilm on the counter, a salmon quiche she had made the day before. 'I ran into your father yesterday. The face on him, the big lug! Enough to scare a ghost away!'

Perched on the bar stool, Isaac was finishing the plat du jour. *Kig ha farz*, a hearty Breton stew of meat and vegetables with buckwheat dumplings, had whetted his appetite; the intense, intoxicating smell alone was enough to reconnect him with a certain sense of pleasure.

'He's not getting any sleep at all. I hear him wandering around the house at all hours of the night.'

'Well, take this – at least this way he'll eat something.'

From out on the terrace, a voice called to Madenn for cider; she nodded to say she would be right there, grabbed a flagon, went outside, filled the glasses and joked with the customers, laying her hand on a shoulder, gregarious and friendly, delighted that she could still cook and wait tables, because it was through her work that she managed to do what life demanded: to connect with other people. Isaac, meanwhile, cleared his plate and, taking the salmon quiche, slipped out of the restaurant and headed home.

No one was surprised when the sunny spell ended and the sky grew dark, reminding the diners that winter was not yet over. From the leaden light, Isaac could tell that a rainstorm was brewing and quickened his pace. Coming to the crossroads, he took the coastal path down towards the sea. Below him was the vast expanse of beach, the sand as white as flour, dappled with dark streaks of kelp and the rocky scree left uncovered at low tide. He hurried on; the rain had just begun to fall, and fat drops landed on the clingfilm-covered plate.

To his right, the ground sloped upwards towards a promontory that stood three metres above the sea. He was about to walk past, to hurry home before the worst of the downpour, when suddenly, without knowing why, he turned and gazed at the headland, though for ten years now he had taken no pleasure in looking at the scenery, for ten years he had not watched the dawn break nor the sun set. The rain was heavy, soaking his hair, streaming over his hands, but he did not feel it. His eyes did not even blink. Almost in spite of himself, he left the path and made his way up to the headland, reluctantly drawn to the thing that had caught his eye; there, on the edge of the cliff, this thing that had appeared to him despite the driving rain, despite the fact his head was spinning with an unfamiliar giddiness. Isaac stopped in his tracks and his eyes grew wide with wonder, like a small child, as he stared at something he had never seen here before, something he had never seen anywhere; and forgetting that he was holding the plate, his arms went limp, the plate fell from his hands, and the quiche smashed into pieces at his feet.

Hugo stood in front of his bookcase and hesitated; he took down a book and reread the back cover. The house was quiet. His parents had gone to Morlaix to take his sister to a medical appointment and would not be back before the evening. Julia had been sulking all morning. She had even pretended she was running a temperature to avoid having to go to the hospital; she hated the windowless corridors, the doctors in their white coats, the endless coughing, the squeak of wheelchairs, this place of sickness and suffering that became a part of her as soon as she walked through the doors. Hugo put the book back, took another one, and half-heartedly flicked through the pages. Isaac Asimov was probably a bit too complicated, Albert Einstein was too well known, and he had already dismissed Isaac Newton – too old-fashioned. Again, he hesitated and went back to one of the books he had already put on the pile. He had never given anyone a book before and was only now realizing how much was at stake: giving someone a book was like confiding a secret.

He picked up *Cosmos*, the first book by Carl Sagan he had ever read, the first book he had read about astrophysics, the one that had opened the way to all the others, and decided that this was the one: the book that had first fuelled his passion. Taking it, he went downstairs and headed off, out through the back gate, shooting the bolt behind him. His house marked the end of the road, the last inhabited place on this part of the island; beyond it, there was nothing but the coastal path that led to the desolate easterly point. He walked along the dirt track, gripping the book so tightly his fingers left an imprint on the cover.

At the foot of the hill was a house that stood apart from the others: the paint on the faded doors was peeling; damp had left traces of black mould on the outside walls; a dislodged roof tile lay amid the unkempt grass. It could easily be mistaken for an abandoned home but for the fact that the lights came on every night, and Alan and his son could sometimes be seen furtively creeping out of the house, like ghosts, oblivious to the fact the building was crumbling before their eyes, aware only of the absence that lived alongside them. A little breathless now, Hugo climbed the front steps and did not even have time to knock before the door opened: standing on the threshold, Alan looked the boy up and down. He was sure he had seen this lad before; he was the son of the new neighbours – or was that someone else? He wasn't certain. No sooner did he see a face than he forgot it; although he did not realize it, he shared his son's lack of interest in the world.

'Hello, I'm Hugo. I live at the end of the road. I've got a book for Isaac.'

Startled at the idea that someone had come to visit his son, Alan said in a gruff voice that he was upstairs in his room. He took a few steps towards the road, then hesitated, turning back to the boy whose name he had already forgotten.

'Was Isaac with you yesterday?'

Yesterday. Shortly after the rainstorm, Isaac had come home sopping wet, his eyes wild, unable even to respond to his own name; leaving a trail of puddles in the hallway, he had headed straight up to his room and Alan had not dared to follow, or even to question him. He had lain awake all night, convinced that there had been another incident, that Isaac was being bullied again, that he had been threatened, maybe even assaulted, and hadn't known how to defend himself, and that he – the boy's own father – wouldn't have known how to help him either.

'No, I haven't seen him for a couple of days.'

The man nodded abstractedly, his head teeming with confused thoughts. Hugo watched him walk away, astonished to see in this father a helplessness he had never noticed in his own.

Three knocks on the bedroom door. The taps were so faint that at first Isaac did not hear them; sitting on the bed, his legs drawn up against his chest, he was staring at his room without seeing it. When dawn streamed through the skylight, he had not known whether he had slept at all during the night. The clothes he had been wearing the day before were drying on the back of a chair next to the radiator. Then three more knocks, louder this time. The door half opened and Hugo shyly appeared in the gap, like a creature come from the outside world to remind Isaac of reality. Nervously, Hugo stepped into the room.

'Remember when we were talking about the planets the other night . . . Anyway, this'll explain things better than I can.'

His hand proffered the copy of *Cosmos*. Hugo longed to say that this was the first book about astrophysics he had read, and that although it was a bit dated now, it was still essential to an understanding of the universe; to say that science was much more than a jumble of theories and computations incomprehensible to the amateur, that it contained a fundamental poetry, that it was the first, the earliest language, the one that linked man to the universe, and that astronomers like

Carl Sagan possessed something truly precious, an understanding of the vastness of things. But Hugo did not say any of this: though he trusted the boy he had come to see, he also felt strangely unsettled by his presence.

He glanced around. Unlike his own bedroom, the walls here were bare. A few exercise books were piled up on a little table that served as a desk. Damp clothes were drying on the back of a chair. In a frame on the bedside table was a photo that he could not see. The furniture was rudimentary; it gave no clue to the person living here. Sitting cross-legged on the bed, Isaac skimmed the chapters, instinctively flicking through the pages. Seeing the boy bent over the book, not saying a word, Hugo realized that he'd made a mistake; that he should never have brought the book, that his hobbies interested no one but himself – after all, who in their right mind would be interested in the countless worlds beyond our knowledge? Suddenly, he was sorry he had come, let himself into this room without being invited, where Isaac was not even looking up at him. Hugo stood at the foot of the bed, feeling awkward and self-conscious. Head bowed, he turned towards the door, vowing to forget Isaac and never to set foot in this house again.

'But if you believe in science, that means you can't believe in God.'

Silence enveloped the room. Sitting on the bed,

Isaac had closed the book and was gazing intently at the cover, as though the book spoke to him more than Hugo could have imagined. 'Everyone at school knows your father is pretty religious. He says he's never missed mass in his whole life.'

Isaac shifted forward, sat on the edge of the bed and looked at the boy standing frozen in the doorway: in the pale face he saw the same suffering he saw in his father.

'But what about you?' he continued. 'You spend all your time reading science books. You believe only in the things we can see?'

It was a question that no one had ever asked Hugo. One that had not even occurred to him personally. He shoved his hands in his pockets and frowned as he gave the matter serious thought, because arriving at an answer would take time. It was true that his father had never missed Sunday mass. That he had had his three children baptized within a week of their birth because any life worthy of the name began in that moment, when a priest sprinkled them with holy water and traced a cross on their forehead. The moment he entered primary school, Hugo had been signed up for catechism classes; he had recited the psalms, repeated the lessons unthinkingly – but also obediently, because at that age, education was not something to be challenged. The rift had come in the form of a book, the very book he had brought Isaac. It was the poetry – the poetry of the vast infinite – that spoke to him. The Big Bang Theory rather than the allegories of Genesis. The great feats of science rather than the miracles of Christ. The death of a star was more fascinating than the lives of the saints. His decision had come to him instinctively as he read, and it had never occurred to him to compare and contrast the two worlds. He had never thought that scientific writing needed to be judged against holy scripture: anything that inspired wonder was worthy of study.

'Scientists are still trying to work out what makes up 95 per cent of the universe. We know that it exists, in the form of matter and energy ... we just don't understand exactly what it is. Science has mysteries of its own. I've simply decided to study those, rather than the Rosary.'

There were other doubts, too. The dark expanse of the infinite, in which there were no certainties. The cutting edge of science, teeming with unanswered questions.

Isaac got up and nervously paced around the room. He longed to confide in Hugo, to tell him what he had seen on the little headland the night before, seen as clearly as he was seeing Hugo right now; but the more he thought about it, the more he began to doubt, to wonder whether his mind had played tricks on him, whether it had been a daydream, an illusion created by the rain and the shifting light. In the end, he said nothing, deciding to embrace his denial, for the mind is always prepared to doubt the truth.

'I think it's brave, accepting the unknown.'

'The way I see it ... that's the one place you can truly find yourself.'

Hugo feverishly gripped the door handle, not daring to prolong the conversation; he sensed that the path to real intimacy lay in the words they were sharing, in the vastness they had fleetingly touched, and this feeling, this rapturous, delicate feeling that would never come again, was both thrilling and terrifying. He flashed Isaac a smile that said he was not abandoning him, that he was only going back to his house at the end of the road, that his friendship was always there if ever Isaac needed it. Then he gently closed the door.

Suddenly the room felt empty. Rain was lashing at the window, and only now could Isaac hear it. He hauled himself on to his bed and poked his head out of the skylight.

Down below, Hugo was walking up the road; beyond his dark silhouette, the shore, glittering with pure white sand, cut into the coastline.

Gripping the frame of the skylight, Isaac hoisted himself up and stared at the point directly opposite: the little headland was deserted.

The last remaining customers had finally left. Chairs were pushed behind the tables with others stacked upside down on top of them. The freshly mopped floor still glistened. Behind the counter, Madenn slowly peeled off her rubber gloves. She was exhausted. A party of twelve celebrating a birthday had stayed late into the afternoon, and what with all the comings and goings, taking out more jugs of cider and more glasses of beer, she had not had a minute to sit down. She glanced at the clock: 5 p.m. Isaac had still not shown up. When he hadn't come by at lunchtime, she had assumed that he was sleeping late and would soon appear, his hair a tousled mess, befuddled by the unusual lie-in. As the hours passed, she had served customers somewhat distractedly, making silly little mistakes, putting too much salt on the steak and not enough on the chips, as she anxiously kept an eye on the road. Now she was pacing the empty restaurant, hands behind her back, her brows knitted in thought.

There had been bad encounters in the past. She had seen Isaac with a black eye, heard the taunts; she had seen other boys pushing him down by the docks and had given them such a tongue-lashing that the whole harbour had heard. Who knew whether the same boys had crossed his path again, taunting and mocking him because he was different. Maybe they had followed him down an alley and . . . The very thought made her stomach heave. She grabbed her scarf and walked out, slamming the door behind her. Outside, the wind had picked up. The trees swayed as she passed, threatening to catch in her hair; a wind that haunted this stretch of road, taking form in every branch, materializing from behind the low crumbling walls, like a voice dogging her footsteps; a changeable voice, now laughing, now stern. But Madenn hurried on without listening; she had heard enough to guess what the wind was saying. When she came to the final crossroads, she passed the dirt track leading to the shore on her right and walked down the road to Alan's house. She knocked on the door, and when she got no answer, she went round to one of the windows and pressed her face against the glass. She saw the empty desk, the jumble of papers, the computer switched off. She was buffeted by a gust of wind; all around, the lawns that sloped down to the sea were trembling beneath this unseen force that only manifested itself through the natural surroundings. Madenn trembled too, and knotted her scarf around her neck. She surveyed the landscape in the waning light, her eyes lingering on a detail far off in the distance. A mop of curly hair. That ash-blond hair, that figure with his back to her – it was him.

'Isaac!'

She raced up the dune, running towards the boy she'd thought she had lost. She called to him again, shouted his name, her words whipped away by the breeze. She crossed the dirt track and arrived at the promontory, but Isaac, standing at the edge, did not react. Arms hanging limply by his sides, he stood motionless, staring at a precise point in the sky. Madenn called his name again, loud and clear. She knew he could hear her now; she was right behind him, only a few steps away, close enough to reach out and touch his shoulder. Lying in the grass at the boy's feet she saw the broken plate, the ruined quiche, flecks of salmon strewn among the pebbles and sand: it was the quiche she had given him the day before. Her heart pounded. Slowly, Madenn walked around the boy, her ankles prickled by the copper-coloured ferns. She stood right in front of him, saw his ashen face, his wide eyes, his expression a mingle of wonder and terror. Once again, she whispered his name, but this time she said it to herself, to convince herself that this was indeed the boy she knew.

A sudden squall sent her reeling backwards and she almost tumbled down the slope. The day was fading fast. A last burst of sunlight spread along the coast, a dense orange glow that dappled the leaves of the trees, burnished the rocks a radiant bronze; meanwhile the sea roiled beneath the wind, malachite green streaked with foam. Everything along the coast seemed to quiver in this last moment, to reach a crescendo on the cusp of twilight. Seeing Isaac standing frozen on the headland, Madenn might have thought he was simply spellbound, dazzled by the vast immensity of it all, moved by this moment between worlds; but she knew that the boy had had no interest in the world around him for the past ten years, that he cared nothing for the twilight or the cycle of the tides, scarcely noticed the full moon. All that Madenn knew for certain was that, in this moment, Isaac was looking at something else. She could not know that he had come to the headland despite himself. That after Hugo left, he had slept for a few hours and then wakened with a start. That, instinctively, without wanting to, he had left his room, his home, prompted by a hand that had guided his steps and brought him here, back to the headland where a day ago he had lost his way, and now could not bring himself to leave.

The church bell tolled half past eleven. Four distinctive notes that rolled through the air all the way to the old port of Roscoff. On the quayside, a latecomer rushed up, frantically signalling to the launch to wait; he ran down the steps to the quay, finally reaching the boat just as the engine began to roar, ready for the off. Looking around for a seat, the breathless man's eyes alighted on one of the passengers: a nun, sitting alone on a bench, facing the porthole, her body straight and elegant, like those ballet dancers who maintain their poise even when not on stage. The launch began to reverse. The sudden movement surprised Sister Anne, and she nervously twined her fingers in her lap: until today, all she had ever felt beneath her feet was terra firma. She slid a little closer to the window, keen to observe every detail of her first sea voyage, full of the innocent curiosity of a child discovering what it means to travel. The boat backed up to the entrance to the harbour, then slowly wheeled around, turning its stern to the lighthouse, and set off. To the left, the breakwater loomed above the sea, stretching out, vast, interminable, until it seemed to meet the horizon, where it plunged headfirst into the water and disappeared beneath the waves, making it impossible to tell where the land ended and the sea began.

Now the boat was gliding between two landmasses. Roscoff, to the left, was framed against the light, the dome of the church soaring above the town, the rocky coastline barely distinguishable from the houses; to the right the wild easterly coast of the Isle of Batz, with its pristine beaches, its slanting trees buffeted and beleaguered by storms. Inside the cabin, all that could be heard was the sound of the engine, a continual throb that lulled the body to the rhythm of the waves. At length, Sister Anne turned away from the window: the blinding reflection made it impossible to look at the sea for any length of time. She closed her eyes and waited for the shimmering afterimage to fade. *It came to me in a dream last night* ... She repeated the words in her mind, her hands lying limply in her lap, one side of her face illuminated by the sun, remembering the voice of Sister Rose: *You'll witness an apparition of the Blessed Virgin in Brittany.* Passengers turned to look at her, as people often do with nuns, their curiosity tinged with deference, as though certain mysteries were no longer mysteries to those who had renounced the world.

The sound of the engine changed, and the launch slowed as it sailed into the island's harbour: all around the bay were the pale facades of slate-roofed houses standing cheek by jowl, vying for a narrow ray of sunlight, as though proximity were the only way to survive on this island. The launch moored at the quay and the passengers got up, retrieved their belongings from the bow: trolleys and pushchairs, shopping bags and sacks of cement, suitcases and bicycles. The two sailors lent a hand as they disembarked, straddling the water and the land, their faces weather-beaten by the wind and the cold. One had pale blue eyes, bleached by the water and the salt; the other had eyes as dark as the deepest ocean where no light could penetrate. As she stepped on to solid ground, Sister Anne swayed for a moment, caught in the rolling motion.

'Sister Anne!'

The Bourdieu family had come to meet her: they had repeated their earlier invitation, insisting that she come to the island, and since her vocation included the pastoral care of the island's parishioners, Sister Anne had agreed to visit on her day off. She said hello to Michel Bourdieu and his wife, kissed little Julia, and then they climbed into the car and drove away from the port and the milling islanders. As they drove, the paved road gradually gave way to a dirt track. Swerving now and then to avoid stones and potholes, Michel drove through the dunes to the last wooden gate; the track came to an end just outside their house. As she got out of the car, Sister Anne saw the silvery shore below and was amazed by the shallow, almost transparent water that seemed at once green and blue – she had heard about this colour, known in Breton as *glaz*, but only now did it reveal its extraordinary character; it seemed less a colour than an enigma. The Bourdieus invited her inside. Theirs was an austere house, decorated here and there with a crucifix or a religious icon; Sister Anne had seen less spartan monks' cells. They sat down to lunch, and together they said grace; the presence of Sister Anne seemed to lighten the mood, and everyone smiled as they reached for their plates and chatted cheerfully. Even Hugo was grateful for her presence here, since it distracted his father. They had had few visitors since coming to the island, and any guest was something to be celebrated. After a dessert of apple tart, Michel Bourdieu solemnly laid his hands on the tablecloth.

'And now, as we promised, it's time to show Sister Anne around the island.'

They trooped out and headed east, up the narrow coastal trail flanked on one side by a row of Lambert's cypresses and on the other by a fence. Brushing aside stray branches that lay across their path, they walked briskly in single file, pushing the pace a little so that they could reach their destination more quickly: from time to time, they caught glimpses of the sea below; the small beaches of fine sand dotted along the coast; the rocky coves that tumbled into the sea; the houses built to face the sun and sheltered from the wind by the bushy cypresses.

'It would have been nice to show you the Delaselle garden, but unfortunately it's closed for the winter. It's a botanical garden, just on the other side of that fence.'

Stimulated by the presence of the nun, Michel Bourdieu suddenly became garrulous. As he led the procession, with his daughter sitting on his shoulders, he proudly pointed out that there was not a single scrap of litter to be seen, that this glorious wilderness was unsullied by man.

'The Breton people don't treat nature with contempt, they revere and obey it. They still have a keen sense of the sacred.'

And it was important to revere and to obey, to recognize what was sacred, to tend towards the divine – and it was precisely because modern man had forgotten such things, had embraced the secular in the vain pursuit of freedom, that society was on the brink of collapse.

'A society that does not venerate anything is not *free*. It is sick, you understand?'

Gradually, the landscape unfolded to reveal sunlit uplands, the paths criss-crossing the meadows, a deep cobalt blue below that dazzled the eye. They stopped for a minute to catch their breath. Michel Bourdieu's mood suddenly darkened as he surveyed this boundless space, terrified by all that he could not see, all that scripture had foretold; he was a scholarly man – he had studied the Gospels and the prophets – but more than this, he had seen enough of the world to known that catastrophe was imminent. In that moment, he was no longer severe. There was nothing intimidating about the heavyset build, the broad shoulders, the hands that could both create and destroy. Michel Bourdieu was a man possessed by fear. He felt a hand on his arm: his wife, sensing his distress, interrupted the gloomy thoughts that so often took her husband from her. The gesture soothed him; he gripped his daughter's ankles, clinging to the child, because this was how he survived, how mankind had always survived: by holding on to the unchanging constant of marriage and children.

They sat on the grass. In the distance some horses were grazing. The path followed the coastline, tracing sinuous meanders before disappearing beyond a rocky outcrop. Not a soul passed by. The island cast its spell on everyone.

'What's that thing around your neck?'

The little girl was staring at Sister Anne's pendant

as it glinted in the sun. She had noticed it while they were walking, a small medal that seemed to protect the nun's every step.

Sister Anne unfastened the clasp and gently handed the object to the child.

'It's a Miraculous Medal. It was first given to Saint Catherine Labouré. She was a Daughter of Charity, like me.'

She told the girl how Sister Catherine had decided to take the veil on 19 July 1830 after the Blessed Virgin had appeared to her one night, when no one else was around, in the little chapel of the Daughters of Charity at the Mother House on the Rue du Bac – the same convent where Sister Anne had taken her first steps in the religious life. It was later described by Saint Catherine as the gentlest, sweetest moment of her life.

'So she saw the Blessed Virgin, like Bernadette did at Lourdes?'

'Exactly.'

The Virgin had appeared to the young novitiate on two further occasions, and during one of these visions she had asked Sister Catherine to create a medal just like the one Julia was now holding, promising that 'All who wear it will receive great graces'; no sooner was it created than the medal was in demand all over France.

The little girl silently studied the medal in the palm of her hand: on one side was the Blessed Virgin standing upon the earth as though watching over the world, her head crowned with a halo, rays of light streaming from her half-closed hands; on the other side was a circle of twelve stars, a large letter M surmounted by a cross, and below the stylized Sacred Heart of Jesus crowned with thorns and the Immaculate Heart of Mary pierced with a sword. Gently, thoughtfully, the girl stroked the symbols with her finger, as though this were one of those magical objects that fascinate the pure of heart.

'So, if you wear it, does it work miracles?'

It was true that miraculous cures had been reported during the cholera epidemic in Paris. A Jewish man named Alphonse Ratisbonne, who wore the medal, had a vision of the Virgin and converted to Christianity, which was much talked about at the time. When Catherine Labouré died, a child who touched her coffin was suddenly cured of a lifelong infirmity. And then there was Catherine Labouré herself, whose body was exhumed sixty years after her death and found to be utterly incorrupt.

'It's not the medal itself that's miraculous ... Nobody ever questioned what the young novitiate said about her visions. It is only when you cease to doubt that miracles can happen.'

The little girl found the story unsettling, though she did not know why; she did not guess how much power these words would have over her imagination. She looked at the nun sitting on the grass, her back turned to the sun, her slender figure bathed in light – she found her somewhat frightening too.

'What about you? Have you ever seen the Blessed Virgin?'

The artlessness of a child, always wedded to a keen instinct. Sister Anne smiled gently and whispered that the Blessed Virgin would always come to those who prayed to her.

They sat for a while, gazing at the coast, then set off home. Their limbs were tired, but it was the pleasurable tiredness of being in the great outdoors, up on a hill with nothing to block the view, where every breath filled the body with a sense of wellbeing.

Before Sister Anne left, the whole family kissed her goodbye as if she were a long-lost friend, and made her promise to come back soon. She got into the car next to Michel Bourdieu, and they set off down the track in a cloud of dust.

At the foot of the hill, a teenage boy suddenly appeared. Sister Anne was struck by the boy's delicate features, by the anxious darting of his eyes, by a gracefulness she had never seen before; looking at him in the rear-view mirror, she asked Michel Bourdieu whether he knew this boy.

'That's Isaac. He's one of my second-year students. Not what I would call a well-adjusted lad.'

The teenager waited until the car had disappeared over the brow of the hill before carrying on his way.

He strode quickly up the dune, crossing the coastal path and making his way towards the headland; he walked on, oblivious to the fact that he was being observed by Madenn, who was standing near the hedge at the top of the path. She had been watching for an hour, perhaps two, her heart pounding fretfully, waiting for the boy to come back to the promontory where she had left him the day before.

When the wind had become too cold, she had walked away without calling out to Isaac one last time. Afterwards, she had been unable to sleep so she had dug out some old family albums; as she leafed through the pages, she had found photographs her mother had kept: the black-and-white shots of four smiling girls – Jacqueline and Jeanne, Nicole and little Laura – had been taken back when her mother was living in L'Île-Bouchard. Her mother had known the four schoolgirls, had witnessed their delight when the Blessed Virgin together with the Angel Gabriel had appeared to them in the village church several times over the course of a week. Sitting up in bed, in the glow of the bedside lamp, Madenn had studied the frank smiles of these country girls, the four innocent faces who had been given the gift of grace; she leaned back against her pillow, the album open in her trembling hands: the next day she would know for certain.

Now, out on the headland, Isaac seemed to be waiting for something. He kept looking around him as though unsure what he had come there to find. Madenn decided to go to him: she approached slowly, step by step, holding her breath, never taking her eyes off the boy. Suddenly her heart began hammering so fiercely she thought she might faint: Isaac had just turned round and gone utterly still, staring at whatever had called him to this place again. Madenn raced back down the path and across the dunes to Alan's house, and as she had the day before, she pounded on the door as if determined to break it down. Finally, it opened.

'You need to come with me.'

She grabbed Alan's wrist and dragged him out so forcefully that he almost fell flat on his face; then she set off at a run. She was already panting for breath and dizzy from the scene she had just witnessed, but she did not slow down; in fact she ran faster, determined that this man should see what she believed to be true.

'My mother was living in L'Île-Bouchard when those visions happened ... She saw the girls in church ...'

Her mother had described the scene in detail: four little girls kneeling at the foot of the altar, motionless, spellbound, gazing up at a blank wall as though it had revealed all the mysteries of the universe, and behind them a group of villagers, seeing nothing yet feeling everything, realizing they were not alone, that in that very moment, the Blessed Virgin walked among them in their little church.

'There was something about their eyes, the way they stared ... And your son ... he's doing the same ...'

Alan stopped in his tracks, annoyed that this woman had dragged him out here for no reason, irritated that she had woken him: having come home from work, he had stretched out on the sofa and had instantly dozed off; he hadn't heard his son's footsteps in the hallway, hadn't heard the front door close. Sleep had simply overwhelmed him. For years now, Alan no longer decided when to sleep: he simply waited, lay awake at night counting the hours, never knowing when sleep would come.

During the day he might drift off for a while. Once, while teaching a pupil to navigate, he had fallen so soundly asleep that he did not hear the screams of the panic-stricken student, who had to steer the vessel back to harbour unaided, and had never set foot on a boat again. His wife's death had robbed Alan of his equilibrium, and he had let it go, surrendering himself to whatever each day might bring; he even took a certain comfort in no longer making decisions.

'What's the matter with you, Madenn? What the hell are you talking about?'

The lack of instinct in men never ceased to amaze Madenn; it was her turn to be annoyed now. She turned, took a step back towards him, fixing him with a steely blue glare; she would say this only once:

'I'm talking about people who see the Blessed Virgin.'

Without giving him time to think, or even to consider what she had just said, Madenn dragged him on again. Down below them, the tide was rising, returning to the shore it had abandoned all day long; the kelp had been washed away and now floated among the waves, a viscous ball that the tide would spit out tomorrow when it ebbed.

'Over there. Your son.'

Standing on the promontory three metres above the sandy shore, Isaac was oblivious to the incoming tide, deaf to his father's voice calling his name; he was staring at the sky, watching the scudding purple clouds. Or was he looking at something else – the gulls circling overhead, the waxing moon already on the rise, some special quality of the light that only he could see? Once more his name echoed into the void, into a world of which he was no longer a part, like the dead vainly trying to speak to the living. The sharp salty tang of the sea filled the air; the tide continued its approach, devouring the last shreds of kelp; the waves murmured as they embraced the shore, ringing the coast with a darkening blue as the light waned.

'Isaac!'

The voice was close now, right behind him. Alan raced up, panicked, unable to bear the sight of this motionless figure that triggered some nameless fear in him. He grabbed Isaac and spun him around; he did not recognize this face. This was his son – these were his features: the almond eyes, the slightly upturned nose, the thin, mute lips – yet Alan did not recognize him. The boy seemed like a stranger. Not knowing what to do, he clutched the boy's arm and shook him roughly, as though shocking the body might bring back the mind; as though he had not shaken his son enough, as though this transfixed face were the result of his neglect. Behind him, Madenn screamed, begging him to stop, not to hurt the boy, but Alan did not hear. It was as if nothing could be heard here on this headland, as if it were cut off from the rest of the world. Alan continued to shake the boy, trying to rid him of the stupor that had frozen his face, gripping his frail arms so tightly he could feel the bones beneath the skin.

'What the hell is wrong with you? What are you doing out here?'

Madenn stepped between them, put an end to the assault, just as Isaac seemed to come back to himself. His cheekbones flushed pink, and his lips parted as if he were about to say something. Then his eyes met his father's and, suddenly, tears began to trickle down his cheeks, wetting a face that Alan had never seen cry – not at the hospital after the accident, nor during the funeral, nor at any other time during the teenage years that Alan knew had been miserable. He watched them flow, not knowing what to say, how to reassure this first intimation of grief. Then he heard a whisper:

'I see, Papa.'

His son was smiling now – not mischievously, not disingenuously – he was smiling, and his eyes, wet and gleaming, were filled with an emotion he no longer expected to feel, as he watched the fleecy clouds scud across the sky, stared into the twilight that had a softness particular to this island, gazed upon all the things that he had been missing until now and which were only just appearing to him once more.

'What do you see? Isaac!'

'I see.'

Feeling utterly drained, Alan let go of the boy, not knowing what to do. Isaac threw himself against Madenn and took refuge in her strong maternal arms.

'I see, Madenn.'

'I know.'

She hugged him to her and buried her face in his salt-flecked hair. Beside them, Alan took a step back, a stranger to these two bodies embracing each other.

Gulls wheeled above them, watching the scene without a single cry. After a moment, a peal of bells echoed along the coast: across the sea in Roscoff, the church was striking the hour.

II
THE SEER

The low skies of early morning, more grey than blue, hung over Roscoff, leaving not a chink through which the sun could peer. From all along the old harbour came the clank of mainbrace against mast: trawlers moored, still asleep, their decks piled with crab pots; their steel hulls garlanded with ropes of blue, yellow, green, purple, still sodden from the day before, symbols of the traditional fishing methods still practised here – methods that protected both the fishermen and the seabed they worked. A single crab boat – a *caseyeur* – was leaving port. It cleaved the water, creating gentle eddies that made the mooring buoys bob up and down on the steel-grey surface of the water. To the east, towering above the harbour, Saint Barbara chapel stood witness to the boat's departure. It was a small, white, modest building set high above the tree line; there was no indication that this chapel had stood here for four centuries, mute witness to every boat that went out and every caravel that did not come back, representing the patron saint of 'Johnnies', the nineteenth-century moniker for the onion traders who set off every summer, their boats piled high with crates, to sell their goods in England, and who prayed to Saint Barbara for her protection as they left. No one prayed to her now. Boats left quays without the deckhands bowing or running up the sails as they glimpsed the church. Now they merely used the white facade to get their bearings as they approached the coast.

The *caseyeur* sailed away and the watching chapel of Saint Barbara stood silently by, forgotten by sailors, a patron saint who had become nothing more than a landmark, a relic shorn of all respect by the modern world.

A group of townspeople had gathered in the church grounds and were chatting easily, commenting on the warm weather and the lack of wind. Bags of clothes and cardboard boxes marked *Children's Clothes*, *Jumpers*, *Shoes* were spread out on the lawns. Two tables had been set up to take the collection; Sister Delphine and Sister Anne were busy sorting clothes and talking to those who had brought donations. A layer of grey cloud still hung over the town, and the church – whose appearance changed in accordance with the light – loomed over them like a block of charcoal granite. No one paid any attention to the bas-reliefs carved into the arches of the holy building: the figure of the shipowner standing on the jib of a caravel flanked by two protecting angels as he faced the raging swell. They had forgotten the countless other ships all around the church, the sea ever-present both within and without – on these walls and in the town itself – the sea which was the first denizen of the earth, one that had witnessed every birth and counted all its dead.

'Could you set any of the clothes with holes or stains to one side, Sister Anne? We don't want to give out clothes that are in poor condition.'

Sister Anne duly complied. Dropping a threadbare jumper into a cardboard box, she glanced up at the chapel ossuary a few metres away, one of two that opened on to the parish close and which she had at first mistaken for an ordinary house. She turned away. The only ossuaries with which she was familiar were those hidden beneath the streets of Paris, visible only to those who were prepared to go down into the catacombs to see them. It was a morbid fascination she had never understood: in going to look at these bones, mere mortal remains, mankind strayed from all that was sacred about the body.

She went back to sorting clothes; on the other side of the tables, a man approached then stood, staring at her: a thick-set man with a pronounced limp and hair slicked over to one side, he seemed to be gazing in astonishment at the graceful face he had just spotted. Goulven rarely came to Roscoff now; he no longer knew who was still alive there and who had died. He had met Sister Delphine three or four times, on the rare occasions when he had found himself obliged to take the motor launch, to cross the sea he had avoided since it maimed him. There was no doubt that he missed it – the rolling swell beneath his feet, the wind whipping his face – but he only experienced those things now when he was forced to, and this morning, Madenn had forced him.

He lifted up the heavy plastic bag that she had given him.

'I've got this bag.'

'You can put it over there. Thank you for your donation.'

Goulven did not leave immediately; he wanted to share the secret that Madenn had confided to him, like a child who had discovered the lure of the forbidden. He set down the bag and stepped closer to the nun.

'There's a lad on the island says he sees the Virgin.'

Surprised at his own words, he gave a chuckle, revealing his toothless mouth. At first, Sister Anne did not understand, saw only the glittering, mischievous eyes gazing at her as though they were casting a spell; she tried to back away, but the man grabbed her wrist.

'Seen her three times already, he has.'

'I'm sorry, Goulven, we've got work to do. Go and tell someone else your silly stories.'

Hands on her hips, Sister Delphine looked the ex-fisherman up and down; normally, the islander rarely uttered a word.

'She told the lad to come back today.'

'Well, tell her we said hello. Now, go on! Shoo!'

Goulven turned back to the nun whose wrist he was still holding. He looked at her, felt the goosebumps on her skin quivering under his fingers; he had the instinct of those who had sailed the seas for many years, those who had learned to read the shifting light, interpret a shadow passing beneath the surface. Careful not to hurt or frighten her, he leaned forward and whispered to her:

'It always happens at the far end of the Route de Sainte-Anne.'

He hobbled away from the churchyard and disappeared into an alley. Sister Delphine shook her head sadly as she folded a jacket.

'Now the poor man's rambling about visions of the Virgin Mary. It can't be healthy, living out on that island the way he does.'

Next to her, Sister Anne stood bolt upright, her face impassive, staring at the space that Goulven had just left. She could still feel his hand on her arm, gripping her wrist as though he recognized her, as though she were the one he had come to seek out. Her hands tensed, crumpling the fabric she was holding. A voice came back to her, intoning the same words, like a salutation: *You'll witness an apparition of the Blessed Virgin in Brittany...*

The breeze blew across the headland, grazed the statuette that was held in place by pebbles around the base, rosary beads draped over the small resin figure. The Blessed Virgin stood, her bare feet tickled by the grass, palms raised to receive entreaties, happy with this altar being built before her eyes. Next to her, Madenn was filling a clay vase with water. Her eyes were intent, her movements solemn; she was still shaken by the memory of the day before. She could still feel Isaac falling into her arms, his body chilled to the bone yet somehow weightless, as though relieved of all mortal cares. She had slowly led him back to the house, his room; once in bed, the boy had looked at her, still overwhelmed by doubt, uncertain of which world he should trust: 'She asked me to come again tomorrow.'

Madenn had stroked his forehead until he dozed off. Then she had sat down on the edge of the bed, feeling as if her legs might give way, overcome by an emotion she had never known until this point. Her mother had told the truth – her mother always told the truth, and Madenn had never doubted her, had always believed that her stories were true, but to see what only the heart has known was something else entirely: the Blessed Virgin walking among mankind.

'Madenn!'

Goulven came trudging along the path, his face still flushed from his trip to 'the Continent'. Madenn had knocked on his door that morning, holding a large bag of second-hand clothes, and told him to take them to the church collection in Roscoff. She had also asked him to bring her back a spray of white lilies. 'Isaac sees the Blessed Virgin.' She had said these words naturally, as though stating something obvious, as though no further explanation were needed. Goulven had taken the bag and asked no questions; during his days at sea, he had witnessed things much more improbable than an apparition of the Virgin.

When he reached the headland, panting and breathless, he proudly held out the bouquet.

'Lilies for the Blessed Virgin, just like you asked!'

Madenn turned round, her blue eyes wide.

'You didn't go telling the florist they were for the Virgin, did you?'

'Nope!'

The man shook his head a little too vehemently for Madenn's liking; she took the flowers from him and placed them in the terracotta vase, focusing on each bloom, studying its height and slant, ensuring there was not a single withered petal, since the sacred called for perfection. And as she arranged the flowers, she thought that perhaps She who had promised to return might already be here, watching her prepare these perfect lilies for her arrival, and the thought made her heart beat faster. Below the headland, the tide had receded, revealing the shallows of the beach, the damp sand criss-crossed with rivulets of water flowing back to the sea. Scattered brown rocks speckled the strand like seaweed, as though tossed at random; further out, in the waters of the ebbing tide, the rocks were covered with a greenish moss, like stateless ruins caught between land and water that told the story of these lands and the spirit of their people.

'Here comes his father, Alan . . .'

Alan had just appeared on the path: when he had opened the windows of his living room, he had recognized the two figures standing out on the headland. The previous night he had waited hesitantly until dawn, longing to go upstairs, to shake his son awake and demand an explanation. He recalled the sight of Isaac's face, frozen like a statue, like someone paralysed by shock. He had paced the living room, chain-smoking cigarettes, listening to the ticking of the clock, but still he could not bring himself to go upstairs, dreading what his son might say, dreading the thing he might not understand. No man experiences feelings of inadequacy the way a father does.

Now, here Alan was, looking at the bouquet of white lilies, the little statue of the Virgin in the grass garlanded with rosary beads, the cantankerous old fisherman he usually saw only at lunchtimes, with Madenn quietly tending to her arrangement – both suddenly transformed into disciples, venerating this spot simply because this was where Isaac had stared into the empty air.

'Oh, come on, Madenn, you can't be serious!'

'You saw what happened as well as I did, Alan.'

Madenn reached into her bag and took out two novena candles. Alan simply could not comprehend this devotion. This faith that had no need to see. This conviction that had no demand for proof – or perhaps Madenn thought she had experienced that proof the day before, in Isaac's silence, in what she herself had felt; for some people, feeling was enough. But Alan sided with his senses, believed only in what he could see. Moreover, putting aside the faith that had ceased to matter to him since the death of his wife, what was happening here involved Isaac, and he was determined not to allow this circus to take place in his son's name.

'I didn't see anything and neither did you. Don't project your crazy ideas on to my son.'

'What's happening here is bigger than Isaac.'

Madenn got to her feet and handed Goulven a candle. She faced Alan, standing straight and calm, certain of what she was doing, filled with a confidence that bordered on arrogance, because she *knew*, she understood the divine, she understood all the things that Alan could not yet grasp. In that moment, she looked like one of those sanctimonious sorts who vaunt their faith, who see it as the ultimate virtue, who pride themselves on being better than other people.

Alan took a deep breath and drew on his last reserves of patience.

'Pack up all of this stuff before someone sees it.'

'I'm not taking down that altar.'

'Madenn, I won't say it again . . .'

'No, absolutely not.'

Seagulls glided above the shore, laughing, amused by the scene playing out beneath them. It was a conflict in which there could be no winner, a clash of words that could not be reconciled; faith and denial, between those drawn to the unseen and those rooted in reality. A light drizzle fell on the coast, a linen veil that blurred its contours, and suddenly, behind them, in the heart of this nebulous space, Isaac appeared out of nowhere, like a ghost materializing. As soon as he saw his son, Alan raced over.

'I forbid you from coming here!'

He took the boy by the arm, less roughly than he had the day before, because he simply wanted to be heard, to remind the boy of his authority, to make him see reason, something everyone around him seemed to have forgotten. He took a step closer, his eyes red with exhaustion, and in a whisper blurted out the words he could not contain:

'You draw more than enough attention to yourself already, Isaac.'

At that point, everything happened too quickly for Alan to grasp: Isaac falling to his knees in a trance; Madenn quaking as, with trembling fingers, she lit the candles; a gentle hand being laid on his arm, the hand of a nun Alan had not heard arrive, as though she too had simply materialized, as though on this headland, things had ceased to obey the laws of reality.

Sister Anne had followed Goulven back from Roscoff and had stayed out of sight, watched the scene play out, right up to the moment when the boy fell to his knees. *It came to me in a dream last night* . . . Now, she walked around the kneeling boy, deaf to the prayers of the two witnesses, fighting a feeling of intense vertigo. *I saw it as clearly as I see you standing here* . . . When she stood before the boy, she recognized him: that teenager she had glimpsed the day before, the one she had seen from Michel Bourdieu's car; she clearly remembered the pale, anxious face. A sense of foreboding took her breath away. She reached out a hand and lightly touched the boy's closed eyes with her fingers: his lashes did not move at all. She turned around and, like him, she gazed into the sky, scanning the heavens for what Sister Rose had promised, for what she too was supposed to see: light streamed through a gap in the clouds, illuminating each tiny droplet of rain, creating a shimmering veil that spanned the space and disappeared into the grey sea.

Again, the downpour in the garden. The lawn mired in boggy puddles, the pink tricycle rusting beneath the raindrops. Sister Anne turns away from the window, weary of this drowned garden. In the half-light, the girl is sitting on the edge of the bed. Quietly, Sister Anne steps closer, never taking her eyes off the child who sees nothing but the closed door. Rain drums on the roof, a deafening roar in the darkened room. There is a creak at the bottom of the stairs; the sound of footsteps climbing. Someone is coming. The child stiffens, stares at the door behind which the danger lurks. The door. In one bound, Sister Anne is there, blindly groping in the darkness for a key, a lock. Still the footsteps climb; there is now no other sound in this house apart from the approaching figure which is far more threatening than the rain hammering the tiles, more terrifying than the sky dark with thunderclouds. Sister

Anne searches for a key. Her eyes scan the dimly lit room and she sees the little girl, her face contorted into a howl, a silent scream that may be heard only by the dead, her tiny hands tugging at her skirt, trying to cover her bare legs, to hide this thing she has not chosen. A dull thud outside the door: he has reached the landing. Sister Anne presses her body against the door, digs her feet firmly into the carpet, and struggles against the force taunting her from the other side; suddenly the door flies open, and she is thrown back and left sprawling on the floor. Quickly, she turns over: there, in the doorway, he has come again.

She sat up with a jolt. With one hand she pushed away the duvet, and with the other pulled her nightdress down to her ankles. She sat, gasping for breath. In the murky gloom, the dolls had disappeared from the walls. There was no sound of rain. The door was closed; above it, a simple wooden crucifix. She swung her legs out of the bed and set her feet down on the cold floor. The roar of the sea drifted into her room. She listened to the distant waves, clinging to the sound, trying to root herself in the present. She did not have the strength to get up: some dreams take time to shake off, requiring a patience known only to those who are wakened by the night, those who know they have to bide their time, to leave the world in which the spirit is wandering, to return once again to the body.

After a moment, her eyes were caught by a glimmer of light: outside, one of the streetlamps was flashing, sending a signal up to her window like Morse code. The light illuminated her bedside table; next to the Bible, a statue of the Miraculous Virgin. Sister Anne felt her gorge rise; her hands gripped the mattress. Yesterday. The deserted island. The headland above the shore. The boy who had fallen to his knees. 'Return tomorrow. The multitude will be with you.' These were the words he had reported. The phrases he claimed to have heard. This memory swept away the nightmare, and Sister Anne got up from her bed, struggling to recall every detail: the rapt face, which she had watched waiting for a smirk, a twitch, the slightest indication that might expose this as a sham, reveal that the boy was merely trying to dupe people – out of malice, out of boredom, because he needed the attention.

A shiver ran down her arms; she grabbed her shawl and wrapped it around her bare skin. She paced the room, arms folded, hands gripping the edges of the shawl as if this could prevent her from falling. This teenage boy would not be the first hoaxer; many before him had fooled the masses, claiming the Virgin had appeared to them, whether they were simple crooks or people who genuinely believed they'd had a vision, or devout followers claiming a unique connection with the divine. And every time, the masses allowed themselves to be convinced, deceived by their own hope, by their longing to believe that the Virgin was always watching over them: She who interceded where men failed.

Outside, the streetlamp stopped flickering. Sister Anne moved through the shadowy room and knelt before the small bronze statue of the Virgin, whose palms were open, inviting prayer: She, the most humble, most merciful; She who appeased all sorrows even before they were spoken. Sister Anne tried to say the familiar words but failed. Again and again her mind repeated: 'Hail Mary ...' but her voice remained silent. She had failed to detect any deception yesterday. She had hoped to expose the boy, to remind him that it is wrong to mock that which is sacred, to simulate faith as though it were a matter of choice. She had said nothing. She had *seen* nothing but the pure radiance of his face, and an inexpressible pain had begun to tighten around her throat.

In that damp room where night had woken her, she remained on her knees, her throat obstructed by that pain, unable to speak to the one who had chosen to appear to another.

'In other news, residents in Plouguerneau had an unpleasant surprise when they were awoken in the early hours by an earthquake. Measuring 4.6 on the Richter scale, it was a particularly powerful quake for the region. This follows an earthquake off the coast some days ago which could be felt as far away as Brest...'

Hugo set his fork down on his plate and turned towards the television: on the screen, people were giving accounts of the dawn quake, talking about picture frames that had fallen from walls, the beds that had moved as though the devil himself were shaking them, the family china found smashed on the kitchen tiles; but mostly, they talked about the noise, the thunderous rumble of the earth that they could still hear even now. Hugo glanced at his parents.

'Plouguerneau... that's about an hour from here.'

At the head of the table, Michel Bourdieu eyed his son scornfully; he often looked at Hugo as though seeing him for the first time, having to remind himself that this boy was his son.

'So what? Did it wake you up this morning?'

He was bothered by Hugo's response and, without saying a word, he took another bite of roast lamb. His younger son inspired a hostility in him that he could not fathom. Perhaps the boy's temperament was too different, his sensibility too refined. It lacked the grit he felt was necessary in a man. He had tried to cherish the boy, tried to see the qualities in this son who was utterly unlike him. But the effort had been too much for him; some children were to be tolerated at best.

'The ground shakes a little here. It's nothing to worry about.'

He was no longer looking at the boy, but his tone was gentler, almost an admission that he regretted his earlier harshness. In the background, the local news was followed by the weather report.

'When are you coming back, Papa?'

On the other side of the table, Julia was staring at the suitcase that had been brought downstairs into the hall. Their father was leaving to attend the funeral of the priest who had officiated at their wedding in the basilica of Notre-Dame-des-Victoires in Paris.

'The day after tomorrow. I'll be on the first boat back to the island. Now eat up your green beans.'

This command vexed the little girl; with the tip of her fork, she speared the beans she had buried under her mashed potatoes, vowing to hide them better next time. The doorbell rang, and Michel Bourdieu got up and left the dining room.

Outside, one of the parishioners took off his beret when Bourdieu appeared.

'Michel . . . have you heard?'

Realizing that the news had not yet reached Bourdieu, the man took a step closer.

'There's a boy who claims to have seen the Blessed Virgin. Here. On this island.'

Michel Bourdieu glanced over his shoulder to make sure no one could hear. He leaned against the doorframe.

'Who is it?'

'The son of your neighbour, Alan. You know, the widower . . .'

'I know who you mean.'

'Four times he's seen her, apparently. They say she's spoken to him!'

Michel Bourdieu looked at the house that sat at the base of the hill. It was so derelict that when he'd first seen it, he had assumed no one was living there.

'I need to go away for a couple of days. I'm sure it won't come to anything.'

'This isn't something we can take lightly, Michel.

This lad is going to have the whole island in a tizzy, and all for a bit of attention.'

The man settled his beret back on his head and walked off. Michel Bourdieu closed the door then stood gripping the handle, staring vacantly at the hallway.

When he finally returned to the dining room, he pretended that François had come round to offer his condolences. He sank back on his chair, surprised to feel a sluggish heaviness overwhelming him. He picked up his cutlery and mechanically went back to cutting up his lamb. The bread was silently passed around the table. Knives and forks clinked. Everyone remained bent over their plates, vaguely listening to the opening credits of an early afternoon soap opera. Suddenly, Michel Bourdieu stopped what he was doing and stared at the son he had only just remembered once more.

'Are you friends with Isaac? The lad who lives at the end of the road?'

Hugo stiffened in his chair. He racked his brain, trying to work out how he had betrayed himself, what he had done to prompt such a question, since his father was anything but perceptive.

'I'm first in the class for maths and science. I don't have any friends.'

Michel Bourdieu studied the boy, his knife and fork

suspended in mid-air; around the table the rest of the family froze, waiting for his reaction, surprised by the tense atmosphere that had settled over their meal. In the background, the television drama offered a recap of the previous week's episode.

'I don't want to find out you've been hanging around with him.'

The father resumed eating, and the rest of the meal passed without another word. After dessert, the dishes were cleared away and the tablecloth was wiped down according to a fixed routine in which everyone knew their role. Michel Bourdieu gathered up his travel documents, and the suitcase was lifted into the boot of the Citroën. Overhead, the sun briefly broke through the clouds, scattering the sea with glitter.

He drove down the road, slowing as he came to the last house. He considered knocking on the door, confronting Alan about the rumours going around about his son. Obviously the boy had seen nothing: it was all in his imagination; he was simply trying to garner the attention he didn't get from his father. The man had clearly not taught his son to worship Christ and His saints, not to make a mockery of what was sacrosanct, not to talk about things he did not understand. Michel glanced at his watch: the matter would have to wait until he got back. So preoccupied was he by this single thought, as he drove up the hill, that he failed to notice the figures walking down the path on the far side of the dune.

There were other people gathered on the headland. The rumours had been spreading through the town since dawn: 'Did you hear the latest?' 'She has appeared among us.' 'The boy's not been right in the head since his mother died.' 'Have you ever heard such drivel?' 'Well, I think he's telling the truth.' 'We should take some votive candles up there.' People bowed over the statuette of the Virgin that Madenn had placed there the day before; they laid white roses, gardenias and sprigs of heather around it; they lit candles, cupped their hands to shelter them from the breeze. Some gazed at the rolling sky, as though perhaps they might catch a glimpse of something. Others stared at the house at the bottom of the hill, watching for the arrival of the boy whose name had been on everyone's lips since daybreak.

'Isaac.'

Alan said the name for a third time. Standing in the middle of the living room, he stared at his son who, despite his insistence, remained utterly silent. Alan had come home in the early afternoon and dragged the boy out of bed, where Isaac had naively hoped he could stay, forgotten. The shutters remained firmly closed; Alan had shut them the previous day, unable to comprehend what was happening outside, blockading his home against whatever lurked there.

'What's been going on out there these past two days? What is it you *think* is happening on the headland?'

The same questions, over and over for more than an hour now. The clock marked out the seconds with an old-fashioned tick-tock. Only a fragment of daylight managed to filter through the closed shutters into this accursed living room, where two shadows faced each other – one standing, gradually losing his patience; the other sitting on the sofa, mute, caught up in memories of the previous day.

'Talk to me, Isaac!'

'I see a woman.'

The teenager spoke softly, as though he could see the woman he was talking about even as he spoke, as though he needed to whisper out of respect for her. Alan wondered whether he had heard the boy correctly, if this whisper was really an answer; it was certainly not an explanation.

'I was there. I didn't see any woman.'

His son seemed untroubled by this detail; he looked serene as he sat on the sofa, patiently waiting for this interrogation to end. Something had changed in the boy, and Alan did not quite know whether it was his bearing, perhaps his voice, or his way of inhabiting silence without worrying about it.

'Isaac, if you're lying to me . . .'

'I'm not lying.'

The doorbell rang. Annoyed by this interruption, Alan left the living room. He moved uncertainly, grumbling to himself. Once again, he had not slept during the night, and he had eaten very little: for the past two days, his routine had been turned upside down, and he still did not understand why.

On the threshold, he found Madenn, who had quickly wiped away the tears from her moist red eyes before the door opened. She no longer saw anything of the boy. Over the past few days, Isaac had stopped coming to the restaurant, had stopped coming to sit at the counter and have lunch with her. Of course, she had seen him on the headland, but there he was caught between worlds and barely able to speak, oblivious to everything around him. Now, the empty stool at the counter, the meals she did not serve him, this absence she had never anticipated, marked a break with happy times she was not sure would ever return.

'I just wanted to ask how he's doing.'

Standing in the doorway, Alan glanced around Madenn, suddenly mistrustful of the island and its inhabitants. Then he leaned towards her.

'My son didn't say that he saw . . . who you're saying he saw.'

The comment amused Madenn, which somewhat alleviated her sadness. She pulled her cardigan tighter around her to ward off the cold.

'He doesn't need to tell us what he sees.'

Suddenly, her eyes lit up as she saw him coming to the door, this boy she had given up hope of seeing, this child she could not have loved more had he been her own flesh and blood. She opened her arms wide and hugged the frail body, thanking Heaven for not taking Isaac away completely, for leaving a little of him for her.

*

Dusk softened the light, revealing deeper, more tender shades; the particular hour when the sun blessed the coastline just before it set. Madenn and Isaac hurried off, huddled together, walking in step, and Alan watched them go, not knowing who was supporting whom, unable to prevent them leaving or to summon the strength to come between them. He stood outside his ramshackle house, and the light that filled the space seemed alien; the twilight was usually so familiar to him that he could tell the time simply by its tone, yet in that moment, there was nothing familiar about it.

In the distance, he saw other figures, a dozen or so, gathered on the promontory. They turned as Madenn and Isaac approached, reverently greeting a son who no longer felt like his own.

This evening, Hugo would be the last witness. He was setting up the telescope in his bedroom under the impatient eye of his sister who kept glancing at her watch, reminding him that the moon would soon rise, and they had to hurry. Downstairs, their mother was putting away the dishes. On the radio, the local news headlines. On the rare occasions when their father was away, the whole mood of the house changed, rediscovering a sense of calm that only seemed possible in his absence.

When the telescope had been adjusted, Julia hopped down from her brother's bed.

'Bring it into my room! I've got a view of the shore!'

She was filled with extraordinary energy, skipping down the corridor, momentarily forgetting her asthma; with her father absent, she recaptured something of the carefree spirit of childhood.

In her bedroom, she opened the window wide and breathed in the damp, briny scent she had loved from the first time she had smelled it. She leaned out and peered towards the shore, where a small crowd had gathered.

'Hey, isn't that your friend? The one Papa was talking about?'

It was Isaac; Hugo recognized him immediately. Far below, staring out to sea, Isaac stood motionless with bouquets of flowers at his feet, flickering candles forming a ring of stars around him. The crowd bearing witness, serious and solemn, were gazing at him as though his mere presence were amazing in itself. It was a curious scene, like a vigil that did not seem to be a vigil, an evening mass with no prayers, and Hugo watched, troubled by a bad feeling he did not understand. Beside him, his sister tugged at his sleeve: the moon was rising, perfectly round, casting a diaphanous reflection over the water. On the horizon, a tawny golden streak; the last vestige of the sun that had disappeared even as its counterpart ascended into the heavens – a cycle endlessly repeated, a reminder that on earth everything was a ritual.

Ignoring her brother, who was too preoccupied to hear what she was saying, Julia leaned further out of the window, transfixed by the spectral presence rising above the coast, just as Isaac was transfixed in that same moment, both of them witnesses to a sky that only they knew how to see.

Two coffees were set down on the table. Bundled up in their coats, the regulars hurried to take a first scalding sip. Outside the window, a fine drizzle fell over the old port; a typical February morning, silent and shrouded in mist, the ghostly streets deserted. The only available warmth was that of the cafe and the steaming coffees that they drank slowly.

A chill breeze whipped through the room: on the threshold a nun was holding the door wide open.

'Do you have a phone?'

She sounded out of breath. She wore a long raincoat that fell to her narrow ankles, and the scarf around her neck glistened with tiny raindrops clinging to the wool. The owner, drying a glass, nodded towards the rear of the cafe. The nun let the door close and moved briskly between the tables, her wimple sliding back to reveal chestnut-brown hair. At the end of the counter, she spotted an alcove and in it an old wall-mounted telephone. She picked up the receiver and dialled the only number she knew by heart. Someone at the convent picked up.

'Could I speak to Sister Rose, please? This is Sister Anne. Sister Anne Alice.'

She clung to the receiver with both hands as though fearing the whole place might crumble around her, just as everything had seemed to crumble around her over the past two days – the street suddenly heaving as she passed, like an earthquake beneath the town; her bed plunging into the waves in the middle of the night: ever since she had come back from the island, nothing had been stable.

'Are you calling me because She has appeared?'

At the other end of the line, the cheerful, rasping voice; the same voice she had heard ever since her arrival, reminding her of the encounter that awaited her in this place.

'There is a boy who claims he has seen her, Sister Rose. He lives on the little island, off the coast of Roscoff.'

'I knew it would happen. Praise be to our Most Holy Mother.'

'But you were mistaken, Sister Rose. And you are never mistaken.'

'You just told me yourself that *She* has appeared?'

'But not to me, to someone else!'

Sister Anne had raised her voice and could now feel eyes boring into the back of her neck: she suddenly became aware that she was not alone in this cafe, and her distress, not to mention her rage, were obvious to all. Her cheeks flushed purple. She was unaccustomed to such outbursts; she never gave in to intense emotion. Like all children who had experienced the unbridled excesses of a parent, she had made restraint her chief virtue.

She leaned against the wall in a clumsy attempt to hide this sudden weakness.

'I was there ... But I didn't see her, Sister Rose, I saw nothing.'

On the other end of the line, Sister Rose was silent as she began to grasp the extent of her companion's anguish, and the misunderstanding that had clearly haunted her for weeks. She had not intended to mislead Sister Anne that morning in the hallway. She had simply wanted to tell her about her dream, to confide in someone she had watched grow up and in whom she placed her trust. She had forgotten that Sister Anne had been praying to the Virgin Mary since she was thirteen, that she had been in awe of the grace bestowed upon Saint Catherine Labouré, that she had spent her whole life waiting for her own encounter with the Blessed Mother. How could she have been so thoughtless as not to realize that Sister Anne would hear only what she so devoutly desired?

'My child . . . I never said that She would appear to you.'

Sister Anne stared at the opposite wall, the receiver pressed to her ear. The words came back to her, the words she had felt she understood, the words that had led her here, to North Finistère, to the edge of the ancient County of Léon, and she realized that she had been deceived by the single word – witness.

It came to me in a dream last night – you'll witness an apparition of the Blessed Virgin in Brittany.

Behind her, the hubbub of customers coming in, greeting the owner, ordering coffees or beers; the rumble of the coffee machine, the clink of cups, the shriek of metal as chairs were pulled out. And that was all it took. Sister Anne's whole world was completely capsized. She hung up the phone and walked back through the cafe, her face ashen, her steps faltering. She pushed open the door, saw the ground begin to shift and the mist close in, the mist that contained the soul of every sailor lost at sea, about to swallow her whole.

'Sister Anne!'

A pair of arms caught her as she fell. She could not see who it was, could see nothing but the veil before her eyes; she surrendered herself to the arms that were supporting her, sheltering her from the drizzle. Seated on a bench, she brought a feverish hand to her brow.

'Would you like a glass of water? A little sugar, maybe?'

Next to her stood Father Erwann, with his compassionate gaze and his reassuring smile. There was not a single wrinkle on his forehead, he was completely beardless, as yet untouched by the vicissitudes of time. Behind his thick glasses, the eyes of the young priest possessed a self-assurance common to those who had chosen prayer as a means of connecting to the world. He kept his eyes on her, still supporting her arm, and this attention bothered Sister Anne, as it exposed a lack of decorum that went against her character.

'I just missed the step and lost my balance. There's nothing more to it. We can go now, Father.'

The priest did not insist and released his grip. A cloak of rain enveloped the old port before them. Beyond the harbour, the receding tide revealed wet, grey sand with pleasure boats sunk into its cement-like sludge, their shipwrecked hulls waiting for high tide to raise them up and restore them.

The priest clasped his hands in his lap.

'Sister Delphine will not be joining us. I'm afraid the sea does not agree with her.'

Father Erwann was thinking about his parish. In the past two days it seemed utterly changed. Suddenly, people were crowding into his church, asking him to confirm or deny the rumours that were circulating everywhere – in the shops, in the brasseries, on every street corner and alleyway – that over on the Isle of Batz there was a boy who had seen the Blessed Virgin. Some named the lad as Isaac, the son of a widower called Alan; some claimed that both father and son had been unstable since the death of Alan's wife, that they had become withdrawn, holing themselves up in a house that had been crumbling away for more than a decade. Others disputed this, insisting that they had seen Isaac in a state of rapture that had sent shivers down their spine, something no one could feign. Everyone offered a different opinion, defended the improbable, argued over what was truth and what was falsehood, and it was left to Father Erwann to calm them, to suggest he go and meet the lad himself and try to shed some light on these claims.

'You've seen the boy, Sister Anne . . . Do you think he's telling the truth?'

'It's not for me to judge, Father.'

After a moment, they set off, walking along the deserted shore. Since it was low tide, they would have to walk six hundred metres across the concrete jetty to reach the launch. They stepped on to the pier, which towered several metres above the water and was buffeted by fierce winds. Without thinking, they bowed their heads as they braved the fierce gusts; below them, between the pillars, was a vast expanse of scree, boulders covered with brackish seaweed, the ancient wounds that the coast carried within its memory. They walked on, leaning into the wind, battling the invisible force that impeded their progress towards the boat.

Just before they boarded, Father Erwann paused: in an instant, his face changed and now bore a grave look that Sister Anne had not witnessed while they were sitting on the bench. It was as though he was intimidated by the prospect of the crossing – not physically but spiritually.

'If I'm honest, I hope the lad's not telling the truth...'

He gazed at the island, uneasy about what he might encounter there, overwhelmed by a sense of responsibility he had never envisaged when he took holy orders.

'History tells us that being a visionary is rarely a good thing.'

A pendulum ticked away the seconds, every swing followed by a dull clank that marked each moment of silence in the room. The half-open shutters let in a wan light. A film of dust lay over the shelves; in every corner, balls of fluff lay waiting to be vacuumed up; sand was ground into the wool pile of the threadbare carpet. The house was so neglected, the very walls seemed to be crumbling.

'Tell me, Isaac, is it true that you see the Blessed Virgin?'

On the sofa, with his jacket unbuttoned to reveal the clerical collar that singled him out from the layperson, elbows propped on his knees, Father Erwann sat stiffly, doing his utmost to mask his sense of inner dread.

'I never said it was the Blessed Virgin.'

Isaac settled his hands on the armrests of the chair,

fingers nervously plucking at the fabric. He knew that the circumstances required him to offer up some explanation. The previous day, he had been all too aware of the troubled looks of those gathered on the headland, the hands that touched his shoulder, the prayers whispered as he passed. It was a curious feeling, one he had found so unsettling at first that he had almost turned back home; he did not understand the meaning of the flowers, the burning candles, these strangers he had not invited approaching him piteously, as though he were the bearer of some promise, as though his personal experience now belonged to other people.

'So what is it that appears to you? I mean, you do see something, don't you?'

'I see a woman.'

Standing in the doorway, leaning against the wall, Alan watched his son talk to the priest as though their conversation were completely normal, as though nothing in what he was saying was implausible. All his life, Isaac had stood apart. He had attracted attention, firstly because he had a sad and gentle face, secondly because his mother's death meant that he was someone to be pitied, a boy deprived of a mother's love. Isaac's presence elicited a whole gamut of emotions – curiosity, admiration and pity, but also violence – and, as if it were not enough that he already stood out, that he seemed condemned to be different, now people were suggesting that he had spoken to the Blessed Virgin.

'Can you describe her? Does she speak to you?'

The adolescent looked to be deep in thought, and everyone leaned forward, keenly observing his silence, trying to determine whether Isaac was genuinely remembering something or whether he was pretending, choosing words at random, pleased by the naive interest people seemed to be taking in him.

'"In the past I have already warned . . . The hearts of men are hardened. They forget that Heaven is watching."'

A sudden chime as the clock struck four, a series of notes that echoed in the hushed room, marking the passage of time. Gradually, the sound faded, and silence settled once more over the room.

'Why you?'

She had finally spoken up. Standing behind the sofa, in the shadow of Father Erwann, Sister Anne reminded everyone of her presence; until now she had been utterly silent, waiting with bated breath, mute witness to a confession she could no longer endure.

'Why would the Blessed Virgin appear to you? To *you*?'

She had sensed the feeling welling inside her, coursing beneath her skin, like a fever radiating from the nape of her neck to the tips of her fingers; a deep, dull ache that racked her body in a way her faith had never done. She was finally discovering, finally grasping, what it meant to hate.

'You're not even a believer . . . I'm sure you've never prayed to her.'

'Sister Anne.'

'Such visions must be earned . . . You have not earned this, you don't even want it! *I* do!'

'Sister Anne!'

Father Erwann got to his feet and stared at the nun. He no longer recognized her; the radiant face with its quiet, unfailing serenity was twisted, contorted by some terrible thing the young priest would never have suspected. Almost instantly, Sister Anne turned and fled the place where she had just revealed her sin; only her voice still echoed, her strangulated words, like a curse called down upon this place.

The day had begun to fade. The dusk was muffled by a thick layer of blue-grey cloud. The coast was silent and serene. Lights flickered on the headland; lanterns, candles sheltered from the breeze. Around the base of the statue of the Virgin lay scallop shells, orange-pink, perfectly chiselled ornaments from the sea; here and there amid the grass stood small cairns fashioned from stones, markers of a sacred place. Sprays of lilies, columbines, roses, irises and other flowers were strewn across the patch of ground that had become a shrine.

'He's coming.'

A whisper rippled along the headland: the shadowy figure of the boy had just appeared on the path. All voices trailed away. Candles were held aloft. In the long seconds of hushed silence, Isaac approached, effortlessly moving through the throng of people.

Behind the child, Father Erwann was staring in wonder at the scene, these hands reaching out to touch the boy's curls, the rosary beads held close to hearts. There were soft murmurs and prayers as Isaac slowly passed among them; in the midst of this crowd, he looked frail, too young to understand the searching eyes. He could have turned on his heel and fled this unwanted attention, since even the stoutest soul would baulk at this level of expectation. Yet he walked on, oblivious to their invocations, seeing nothing but the darkening sky. Suddenly, he fell to his knees. Instantly, there came a tumult of cries and jostling bodies as the crowd surged towards him.

'Don't touch him!'

Madenn suddenly appeared and repelled the heaving crowd, ordering them to take a step back. People pushed and shoved, craning their necks to get a glimpse of Isaac. The tightly crammed throng seemed to be in danger of tumbling off the outcrop on to the rocks below at any moment. It looked like every crowd that had ever existed, every horde that had come to view religious ecstasy, to witness a miracle, some proof that the Blessed Virgin still visited the earth, proof that humankind still warranted her grace.

Madenn spread her arms wide to protect the boy behind her. The last light withdrew from the coast, turning the crowd into a dark, quivering mass. Madenn watched every gesture, every movement, keenly aware that nothing was more unpredictable than an excitable mass of people, that a single shout could shatter this fragile balance. After a moment, she noticed a distant figure further along the path: the woman's arms hung limply by her sides and she did not move, as though disdaining to come closer, as though scorning the impassioned crowd. The breeze lifted the veil that covered her hair. Still, she stood, watching from a distance, a frozen shadow robbed of every breath.

The cry of seagulls, close at hand, strangely close; the lapping of waves. The cold was all around. Sister Anne opened her eyes and was surprised to see a pale glow. The only roof above her was the sky; her only bed, a sandy hollow. She had taken a fall. She remembered now, last night: the memory came back to her ... She had fallen into the ditch but had not called out for help. After a time, she had walked away from the headland, tired of the gullible crowd, of the prostrate child. She had carried on walking, hands brushing the tall grasses, not knowing where the dark path might lead her. After a while, the ground had begun to slope steeply and she had descended, feeling the sand beneath her feet, listening to the sea. Then, suddenly, the ground had opened up beneath her and she had tumbled into the darkness.

During the night, she had opened her eyes and

stared up at the clouds as they receded, at the moon, the bluish glow unique to the coast, the starry firmament that she had never seen before, the one that people in cities could never see; the one they had all but forgotten, but which still existed, there, above the tall buildings that blotted out the sky and dulled its radiance. She had wanted to keep looking at it, to contemplate each new star as it revealed itself to her eye, but she had sunk back into unconsciousness, as though death were calling her, here on this bed of fine sand – or she wished it were so, because now that she was awake again, this return to consciousness, this resurgence of memories, filled her with dread.

She sat up. Damp sand stuck to her hands, so she rubbed her palms together and looked around. The pale shore was deserted. The sea was calm and clear, the tide slowly coming in. To her right, rising above the water, she saw the lonely headland, the flowers that had tumbled on to the beach, the melted wax of the candles, the absence of the faithful now that the boy had gone; there was only the little statue of the Virgin, ringed with rosary beads, patiently waiting for the next call to prayer.

Leaning on one knee, Sister Anne got to her feet. Her hair was uncovered; her wimple had been blown off during the night and now floated like seaweed on the surface of the waves. She ignored it and took a few faltering steps, looked up at the sky, gazing into the pale light; she turned back, called out to this desolate place, demanding that she too might *see*. She looked like a madwoman, meandering along this cold shore, her habit crusted with white sand, staring into the heavens, waiting for a response – some sign, however small, that she had not spent her nights praying, had not renounced the world, only for grace to be bestowed on another.

From behind her came the roar of an engine. In the distance, beyond the beach, a battered Citroën 2CV was driving along the track. It stopped outside the house at the end of the road. A little girl rushed out to meet her father as he slammed the car door shut.

'Gently does it, Julia. Remember your asthma.'

Michel Bourdieu lifted the child into his arms. The rest of the family came out to greet him, pestering him for details of his trip, the train there and back, the hotel where he stayed, whether he was exhausted.

'We made the right decision when we left Paris. The city has been ruined by the people who live there.'

Breakfast was made, coffee and hot chocolate, butter and jam, toast and orange juice; the room was filled with sweet scents that told of morning and warded off the problems of the day. There was a knock at the door. The mother, who was always surprised when someone called at the house, set the coffee pot down on the table and went to open the door. On the threshold Sister Anne looked like a ghost, standing straight and pale, as though nothing now inhabited her icy body. She fell into the mother's arms.

'He has seen her . . .'

Though somewhat taken aback, the mother took the nun in her arms, registering all the details that revealed how she had spent the night: the sand in her hair; the damp, frosty cloak. The nun's sobs strangely reminded her of her daughter. Michel Bourdieu appeared at the far end of the hallway; he recognized the voice, even if he did not recognize Sister Anne in the figure standing in the doorway, stripped of her blue veil, her innate reticence, the serene composure she usually presented to the world. In his wife's arms, she was no longer a nun, nor even an adult; she was like a tearful child seeking comfort for some sadness they fear they will never get over.

'This is about the boy, isn't it?'

Michel Bourdieu stepped closer. A mounting sense of foreboding had haunted his entire trip, a bad feeling he'd had ever since he had been told that a boy on the island had seen the Virgin Mary.

The sister looked up at him, her eyes filled with tears.

'It's all true.'

The sobbing had abated. Only a faint, barely perceptible echo still lingered, as though Sister Anne's grief had not quite left the house. The light had changed, become insipid, now that the morning was drawing to a close. A silence reigned over the house, the sort of austere calm that follows an argument, the silence of solitude.

'Could you make me another tartine?'

Julia took a large mouthful of bread, spreading strawberry jam everywhere and leaving her mouth smeared with butter. She ate greedily, dipping the tartine into her milk, untroubled by the morning's upheaval. On the other side of the table, Hugo seemed preoccupied.

'Finish that one first,' he said.

'Oh, don't try to be like Papa. Anyway, you need to eat, too. Your chicory must be cold by now.'

It was true that Hugo had not touched his bowl, unable to swallow, let alone eat anything. He had lost the ease of childhood, when appetite is seldom suppressed by external events. Outside, the Citroën 2CV had driven away; a cloud of dust still hung above the dirt track. *We're taking Sister Anne back to Roscoff. Don't go out. Don't open the door to anyone.*

What had invaded their home that morning was a strange kind of excitement: the distraught nun who had to be consoled, though no one truly understood her anguish; who had to be warmed up, as her shivering body looked as though it might shatter on the floor. She had been served hot tea, dressed in a woolly jumper, and Hugo had stared at the nun who no longer looked like a nun as she sat on the sofa, cupping the tea in her hands, staring into space and repeating the same words over and over: *Isaac, he has seen her, Isaac.* From that moment on, Hugo had been unable to eat, unable to think of anything but the knot in his stomach.

At the sound of the doorbell, he flinched. Sitting opposite him, his sister dropped her tartine and climbed down from her chair.

'Papa told us not to open the door, Julia!'

But the little girl ran out into the hall, curious to see who it was now, surprised by all the strange visits. She opened the door and a beaming smile lit up her guileless face.

'So, you're the boy who sees the Virgin Mary?'

The three figures slowly made their way up the dunes. The island seemed deserted, lashed by an icy wind that clawed at their faces. *A nor'easter*, Hugo thought to himself. He had learned the names of the winds and felt slightly less disconnected from the island now that the invisible had meaning. The tall grasses bowed as he passed. Here, the last sounds of the shore died away, the lapping of the waves, the cries of the seagulls; all those things that betokened the living, the familiar, faded into the distance. They were moving inland, entering a world of whispers and susurrations, a world that was initially intimidating, then gradually comforting, as though the human mind knew these landscapes, recognized the things to which it belonged.

Isaac, who was leading the way, turned back to Hugo and his sister, and suggested they go down to the old chapel. He still hadn't told them the reason for his sudden visit; he had trouble enough understanding it himself. He had knocked at Hugo's door filled with a self-assurance that was unfamiliar to him, surprised that he had been unable to stay in his bedroom.

Falling into step, they walked down the steep slope towards the ruins that rose from the hollow. Ten centuries had put these stones to trial – by storm, by sand, by fire – but still they stood: the arches, the gable windows, the pillars of the nave, the apse that had become a shrine to Saint Anne. The island had encroached upon the petrified church: lush grass carpeted the nave; pennywort sprouted from narrow crevices, the veins and arteries of a body that still breathed; and ivy tumbled from above the northern transept, springing straight from these ancient stones – a lesson that life can burst forth even from decay.

'Look, Julia, that's Saint Pol slaying the dragon.'

Isaac had stopped in front of the rusty gates leading to the altar: on one side the statue of a monk stood on a stone pedestal. He wore his chasuble and carried a stole in one hand and his sacred sceptre in the other; the colours of the vestments had been washed away by the constant rain. Head bowed, he calmly observed the snake he was crushing beneath his feet, the timeless pose of one unsurprised to see faith prevail over evil.

'They say that, once upon a time, the people on this island were terrorized by a dragon...' said Isaac.

According to legend, Saint Pol was summoned to rid the island of the dreaded beast: having no sword and no army, this man of faith trussed the dragon using his stole and dragged it by the neck to the westernmost promontory of the isle before hurling it into a great hole known ever since as Toull ar Zarpant, the Pit of the Serpent, which was today covered with imposing rocks.

'During storms and spring tides, the waves crashing against the rock sound like the dragon's roar...'

As Julia stared at the statue, she could hear the beast's cries, could imagine it imprisoned beneath the rock, still alive, waiting for the day when it would be free to impose its reign of terror upon the island once more. The wind wound itself through the arches, played ethereal notes in the vault of the nave; it was almost as though you could hear the ancient voices that had sung psalms and prayers here so long ago in now-forgotten tongues.

Standing to one side, Hugo could not hear this ancient music. Nor was he listening to what Isaac was saying, uninterested in the island's legends, indifferent to everything that did not relate to the present. He wandered through the ruins, hands behind his back, the same hard knot in his stomach; from time to time, he looked up and anxiously gazed around: some force weighed ominously over these ruins, and he was afraid to discover what it was.

'Did you ask the Virgin for a miracle?'

His sister was staring at Isaac. Until now, she had only ever bumped into him on the road or outside Madenn's restaurant; she had never seen him up close, never seen this face that now held her captive.

Isaac smiled gently at her.

'She did not say who she was.'

'All you've got to do is ask her to perform a miracle – that way you'll know if it's her.'

The little girl nimbly hauled herself up on to a pillar, clasped her hands and thrust them towards the heavens.

'O Blessed Virgin, prove to Isaac that it's really you! Do a miracle!'

'Julia!'

The deep voice rumbled around the ruins, and the girl was so scared that she almost fell off the pillar: at the top of the dune stood her father – the last person she had expected to see – his face a mask of black fury at finding his children here when he had expressly told them not to go out, and – worse – hanging around with this boy whose very name he abhorred. He barrelled down the slope, a great wave crashing down on them, ready to engulf them and obliterate what remained of the ruined church. He picked up his daughter, ordered his son to go home, then turned to Isaac as though he were the devil himself.

'I don't want to see you anywhere near my family ever again.'

The nor'easter whistled though the nave, or perhaps he was just imagining the sound: Michel Bourdieu could see nothing but the ruined church, a broken chancel with a broken cross forgotten by the centuries. He ran from the place, deaf to his daughter's cries, without a second glance at the boy who had filled him with nameless dread. It was as though the world was spinning. He raced back across the dunes and reached his house, panting for breath, weighed down by a burden that did not belong to him. Setting his daughter down, he ran over to his son who was standing at the foot of the stairs and stopped the boy in his tracks.

'You lied to me, Hugo!'

He grabbed his son's arm, ready to snap it in two at the slightest false move, to throw the boy out on to the street if he dared defy him again.

'When I asked if you and that boy were friends, you lied to me!'

'I don't think of him as a friend.'

Hugo spoke without looking at his father; he was calm and composed, proving that he had risen precisely where his father had failed. Michel Bourdieu stared at his son, disturbed by this answer, not sure what to make of it, whether there was some nuance, some subtlety that had escaped him.

His wife laid a firm hand on his shoulder.

'That's enough now.'

She fixed him with a stern glare that Michel Bourdieu rarely saw in her; his wife possessed the terrifying authority that only the kindliest people can muster. Julia was sobbing in her arms, not daring to look at the father who had pushed her around more than seemed reasonable. Michel Bourdieu released his grip on his son; he felt a sharp pain in his fingers. Then everyone disappeared: his son stamped up the stairs and slammed his door; his wife locked herself in their ground-floor bedroom.

Michel Bourdieu stood at the foot of the stairs, gazing around the house in which everyone had fled from him.

This was the time of day when dinner was usually prepared: the strains of banal music from the kitchen, the hum of the oven as it heated up, a baguette being cut into slices, vegetables bubbling in a saucepan, the harmony of hearth and home; all the things that Michel Bourdieu prided himself on having achieved, all the things that he could not hear at this moment. Night stole into the house. Sitting in the living room, he was no more than a shadow on the sofa, stolid and serious, staring around him at a gloomy space in which not a single lamp was lit, in which his daughter's laughter did not break the silence. From time to time, there came a creak, and he would listen, thinking his wife was emerging from her room, thinking his son was coming downstairs to join him. Then the sound would fade, and Michel

Bourdieu would sigh: every man founders when his family bursts apart.

There was a knock at the door. Michel Bourdieu pulled himself from the silence and grabbed his leather jacket. Outside, four men stood waiting.

'Ah, Michel, there you are . . . We saw all the lights were off, so we thought . . .'

One of the parishioners took off his cap and stepped closer.

'I have to warn you, there's a whole crowd up there.'

Michel Bourdieu did not answer; he simply pulled on his jacket and set off. As they headed up the track, the five men felt the icy grip of the wind, that glacial coastal wind that seeks out the slightest patch of exposed skin and chills it to the bone. Each of them steeled himself, pulled up his collar, and focused on the struggle between the body and the elements.

'Over there. On the headland.'

Directly ahead, perched above the shore, the dark mass of bodies buffeted by the nor'easter stared into the dark at the boy Michel Bourdieu could not see. He stopped. Still, he longed to believe that this was nothing, that the gullible masses were mistaken. Surely they knew that every time the Blessed Virgin had appeared on earth, she had prophesied war and catastrophe, had made those visionaries gaze, helpless and terrified, into the pit of hell, witness the death of entire peoples, the end of time itself. Nothing was more threatening to mankind than visitations from Heaven, and only Michel Bourdieu seemed to be aware of this.

'Father Erwann hasn't made a pronouncement yet. I've always thought he's too young; he doesn't understand what's at stake here...' Michel Bourdieu listened half-heartedly to the man's words: the boy was lying, that much was certain, but the crowd was growing, and excitable now; before long this might become an uprising. It was imperative that he put an end to this hoax. Impervious, rigid with a cold feeling he had never known before, he stared at the scene on the headland.

'How do you know he's lying?'

With a leap, Michel Bourdieu darted off down the path. In the distance, candles flickered in a small pocket of darkness just above the shore; Michel crept closer now, a menacing figure in the half-light, crouching low so that he would appear only at the last moment. Then he jumped up and charged into the crowd, causing a commotion that took those present by surprise; there was shouting and shoving, candles were knocked over, and in the sudden confusion, everyone seemed to lose their footing, overwhelmed by this unexpected turn of events. The sea of people parted to reveal the tip of the headland, the lanterns, the stone cairns, the scattered bouquets of white flowers – and the boy, there on his knees, oblivious to the backwash behind him.

Michel Bourdieu launched himself at the child, tried to lift him off the ground the way a raging current tries to move a boulder; but it was as if Isaac were fused to the rock, a granite slab, impossible to shift. Michel Bourdieu seethed as he redoubled his efforts. Suddenly discovering a latent fury, he brutally lifted the boy off the ground, dragged him back into the world, only for another axe to fall, an axe that he had not anticipated – a more powerful, more devastating force that pushed him aside so viciously he almost tumbled off the headland.

'Don't you dare lay a hand on him!'

It was Alan, the father no one expected; Alan here for the first time that day, the widower who now towered over Isaac, protecting this boy who was still his son even if he was stolen away by the coastline each night. The clamour of voices fell silent; hushed seconds while icy gusts mercilessly battered the dazed crowd, as though the violence were everywhere.

'You need to leave.'

Here, on this rocky stretch of coast, Michel Bourdieu was the one being told to leave: it was *he* who was being spurned, just as his family had spurned him earlier. He had sensed his imminent fall that morning, the moment Sister Anne walked through his door, the moment she brought her downfall into his home: no one falls without taking another person along with them.

'When the Heavens visit the earth, it only ever portends evil.'

Michel Bourdieu walked away without a word, without a regret, plunging through the darkness until he melted into the night.

The wind blew across the slate roof. In the bedroom, the lamp briefly flickered. Lying under the covers, Isaac stared at the photo in the dim light: a portrait of a blonde woman, his mother, sitting cross-legged on the sand, hands cupping her swollen belly; all around her, the pristine white shore, blazing in the summer sunshine.

A faint tapping at the door, a creak, and then his father appeared.

'Did I wake you?'

Isaac shook his head. His father shuffled into the room looking slightly awkward. He never came into Isaac's bedroom; he wanted to give the boy his privacy, but also perhaps it was because he was a coward, so this was the first time he had seen the dull, blank walls, the plain table that served as a desk, the cupboard that extended from the floor to the loft bed. It was a spartan room, like a monk's cell, though monks at least had the Bible for company.

'Does your arm hurt?'

'I can't feel a thing. It's as though he never touched me.'

Isaac sat up, surprised to see his father there, just as he had been surprised to see him on the headland earlier that evening. For some days, they had taken to avoiding each other, unable to engage in even the most trivial conversation. Isaac would leave the house as the sun began to set and Alan did not try to stop him. He pretended not to notice, not to hear the front door closing; he felt overwhelmed by what was occurring and could see no end in sight. He knew what happened out on the headland; he could not leave his house without people commenting on it, had seen them look at him askance with a mingle of curiosity and contempt, had heard the rumours circulating all over town. That night, for the first time, he had wanted to see too. He had found the dark, silent congregation gathered on the headland that had become a shrine, seen his son prostrate beneath the sky. Curiously, he had found the scene less disturbing this time: there was a serenity about it he had not noticed before, some kind of conviction that he could not put into words. But then violence had flared out of the darkness, and everything had suddenly changed.

A gust of wind pummelled the window and the

lamp bulb flickered again. Alan recognized the picture frame his son was holding, the photograph he had packed into a cardboard box all those years ago, on the day he had consigned his memories to a dusty storage unit.

'I didn't know you had rescued that photo . . .'

He stepped closer and looked at the photograph he had taken on an August afternoon, on the sandy shore outside their home. His wife had spent much of her pregnancy on the beach; she wanted their son to hear all the sounds that awaited him, the teeming life outside the womb that he would soon come to know. After Isaac was born, she had taught him how to take his first steps on the pristine sand, taught him not to be afraid of the seaweed that clung to his ankles, taught him to spot little crabs so that he did not get nipped; she had taught him to gaze into the distance, to read the world, the ebb and flow of the tide, the changing of the seasons, the cycles of the moon, the rolling sea and the creeping mists, the perfection he should salute and strive to imitate.

'Tonight . . . *she* said to me . . .'

Sitting on his bed, Isaac paused; he seemed deep in thought, as though silently rehearsing the words he was about to say. Meanwhile the wind howled around the house, seeming to die away only to spring back to life, striking the windowpanes so hard it seemed like they might shatter; a fearsome and majestic presence that drowned out all other sound in this cavernous night.

'She said: "To believe is to receive."'

His son smiled serenely, as though finally relieved of his worries, as though he had at long last found what he had been searching for: the end of their grief.

This time Alan did not question him. The truth seemed unimportant: he did not care whether Isaac was being honest, whether he had heard another voice or whether it was his own, whether what he saw was the Blessed Virgin, some other woman or simply a manifestation of his lonely dreams. The ends justified the means.

A little awkwardly, he laid a hand on his son's shoulder – he had grown unused to such gestures of affection – and then he left Isaac's room, hiding a tremulous smile.

Children laughing. Outside, right next to their house, and their laughter woke Julia. Her body drew her back towards sleep. The storm had raged all night, growling and threatening to blow away the roof, to smash down all the doors, while Julia had cowered and held her breath, terrified by the unseen force that seemed to be watching her from outside the window.

There came another burst of laughter, children teasing and calling to each other a stone's throw from her home. She opened her eyes to find a room that was not hers. The walls were lined with flowery wallpaper; the windows were covered by linen curtains. Her mother lay next to her breathing shallowly, one shoulder peeking out from under the duvet. They had fallen asleep here yesterday after they had left her father standing at the foot of the stairs. Julia slipped out of bed and quietly opened the curtains: a ball bounced;

children emerged from the dunes, chasing the foam ball down the slope; the sky was clear and cloudless. Julia tiptoed around the bed and sneaked out of the room without waking her mother.

Outside, the voices grew more distant. Morning wore on and a shaft of sunlight reached through the window, extending from floor to bed, then to the duvet, until it touched the cheek of the sleeping mother, the gentle warmth on her face finally waking her. Seeing that her daughter was gone, the curtains were half open and the door was ajar, she pulled on her dressing gown, padded down the hallway and glanced into the kitchen. She went upstairs to check Julia's bedroom and the bathroom, then came back down to the living room and found her husband lying on his side, his arms folded around him, his knees drawn up, wedged between the armrests of the sofa that was too short for his frame.

'Michel . . . ?'

Michel Bourdieu woke with a start and almost tumbled on to the floor; exhausted and wild-eyed, he noticed his wife standing in the doorway.

'I can't find Julia.'

Outside, the skies were as blue and clear as a spring morning. Husband and wife went out through the gate and headed down the dirt road, taking turns calling their daughter's name. Before long, they heard high-pitched squeals: down on the shore, a group of children were tossing around bits of bladderwrack. All across the beach, huge piles of red and brown seaweed washed up by the storm mottled the once pristine sand. They spotted Julia running around with the other children, blossoming, thriving in this space a city child could not even begin to imagine; she jumped into the slimy heaps with both feet, ducking and weaving in an impromptu game of dodgeball between the mounds of kelp.

The ball flew past; Julia caught it and prepared to throw it at the opposing team.

'Julia!'

Julia was so startled to hear her name that she dropped the ball, which rolled towards the waterline; looking up she saw her mother – a physical barrier between frivolous fun and grim reality. She gripped the girl's shoulders.

'You know you're not supposed to run around!'

Her mother listened for the wheezing that usually preceded an asthma attack; she noticed her daughter's excited face, flushed with unfamiliar colour. Around them, the other children had stopped playing, unsettled by this serious turn of events, as though the grown-up world could not intrude on childhood without shattering it.

'Listen, Maman.'

Julia grabbed her mother's hand, pressed it against her chest: she took a long, calm breath.

'See? No wheezing.'

Julia took another long breath, holding the palm against her ribcage; her mother listened intently for the familiar sound that – logically – should have been triggered by this episode. After all, she had just seen her daughter running along the beach, skirting the waves, dodging and throwing a ball, playing between piles of seaweed, her cheeks flushed, her eyes shining, breathless from an exertion that seemed to have no more effect on her than it did on the other children. She stared at her daughter, puzzled, unable to grasp what Julia had intuited the moment she got out of bed that morning.

'The Blessed Virgin has cured me, Maman.'

III
A MIRACLE

There was a deafening clamour in the restaurant; there was not a single unoccupied table. The diners were crammed together like sardines, others perched at the counter or sitting on folding chairs brought from the kitchen. From table to table, voices were raised; people called and shouted, an unusual, bubbling tumult, driven by the only topic of conversation that had been stirring the island since the morning.

'The little Bourdieu girl's asthma has been completely cured.'

'It was the intercession of the Blessed Virgin, that's what it was!'

'How do we even know she's been cured?'

'The doctor paid them a visit last night. He's completely baffled.'

'What about Estelle Faguette? She had an incurable illness, and the Virgin Mary cured her!'

'Yeah, but that was – what? – a hundred years ago!'

Madenn moved between the tables, serving food, taking away empty jugs. She looked preoccupied. There was none of the usual banter, none of the genial welcome for which she was known. Although the dining room was packed, this was not one of the lunchtimes brimming with the good humour she usually enjoyed: this was an explosive, unsettling furore. Like a bar at closing time when everyone is tanked up and it would only take one word for a fight to break out, the rowdy diners here seemed likely to snap at any moment.

'I've got osteoarthritis – why doesn't she cure me, eh?'

'What about me? I've got cancer!'

'You've been saying that for the past ten years. That's not cancer, it's hypochondria!'

'*Enough!*'

The gales of laughter were harsh and maddening, or perhaps Madenn simply could not stand these people any more. She pushed open the front door, stepped out of the restaurant, and took a deep breath of fresh air. Out on the terrace, diners were huddled on benches, finishing their lunch. She went and cleared some plates, took fresh orders: bread, some quiche, a flagon of *chouchen*.* She couldn't focus; she kept

---

* A drink like mead, common in Brittany.

turning around and anxiously scanning the road. For several nights now she had been woken by the same sound: a dull thud, the sound of a body falling to the ground, a body being beaten and, with it, a rasping guttural breath, the horrid panting of some beast that filled her with a nameless terror. Every night, she had got up and peered out of her bedroom window, blindly groped her way down to the empty dining room, yet outside she saw nothing but the deserted road. This morning, for the first time, she had been truly frightened on her way home from the market; she could sense something lurking in the fields, or at a bend in the road. She had run the rest of the way back, suddenly aware that nowhere on this island was safe any more.

'Have you got chips on the menu today?'

Off to one side of the terrace, sitting at his customary table, Goulven was eating his sandwich with both hands. He seemed untroubled by the boisterous crowd, more interested in his lunch than in some miraculous cure.

Madenn was walking past with a number of empty plates.

'You can see the place is jammed, Goulven. I'm only serving cold dishes.'

'But I have a hankering for a plate of chips.'

Madenn turned on her heel and slammed the plates down on Goulven's table.

'Then cook them yourself!'

She barged back into the stifling dining room. The windows were fogged with condensation and gave off the sour smell of cider. The clamour in the place grew louder as glasses were knocked over, cutlery clattered on to the floor, fists pounded on tables.

'The Virgin has to perform a miracle now. A bona fide miracle!'

'Yeah, something we can all witness.'

'Hey, Madenn!'

A customer grabbed her sleeve, dragged her into the centre of the crowd like a fish caught in a net.

'You know this boy, don't you? Tell him to ask for a miracle!'

'Youenn's got a point. That lad needs to pull his finger out.'

'Too right. He just kneels there on the ground, doesn't say what he sees, and there's us all standing around like lemons!'

A baying pack, yapping at each other across the tables, presuming to talk about the sacred when they had lost every shred of humanity. If God Himself had appeared to them in that moment, they would have wanted more: more proof, more concrete evidence. Nothing had ever been enough for mankind, not since Abraham. Madenn took a deep breath. The pink had drained from her cheeks. Her sweaty hair was plastered to her forehead. She leaned one hand on the back of the customer's chair.

'Get out.'

A whisper rippled around the tables, followed by giggles of disbelief. Then Madenn whipped the chair away, tipping the benighted customer off his seat. Suddenly, everyone fell silent, shocked by what she had done, but mostly surprised by the power in her grip.

'Get out! The lot of you!'

She grabbed one end of a paper tablecloth and pulled it away, sending the crockery crashing on to the floor. Instantly, she moved on; another table, a sharp tug on the tablecloth, smashed plates, shards of glass everywhere. In stunned silence the diners stood up, collected their coats and scarves, pushed their way through the front door, and warned everyone outside that Madenn had gone stark raving mad.

Within minutes, the place was deserted. It was a strange, almost mocking silence of the sort that follows storms that have uprooted trees, capsized boats and then disappeared, giving way to silence, as though nothing had happened, as though there had been no destruction. The empty restaurant now looked like a rubbish tip, with shards of crockery and upturned chairs all over the floor, pieces of quiche and cheese and breadcrumbs scattered everywhere, while tankards of beer spewed out their creamy foam.

Having made sure that no one was left inside, Madenn went out, double-locked the door, and started walking down the road.

Outside Alan's house there was a gathering of the faithful. An incongruous, impromptu congregation stood, humble and reverent, praying, singing hymns, reciting the Rosary in front of the run-down house in which the seer lived. Madenn appeared, striding down the road, gesticulating wildly.

'This is private property! Clear off!'

Surprised and intimidated by this sudden display of authority, the crowd scattered and regrouped a few metres further down the road, where they carried on praying. Madenn climbed the steps and knocked several times.

'Alan! Alan! It's Madenn . . .'

The door opened a crack to admit her. Inside there was no daylight; the hall and living room were steeped in a murky gloom. Alan had stopped opening the shutters when curious onlookers began to press their faces against the windows, trying to catch a glimpse of Isaac in his natural habitat. Alan's house, an unprepossessing building that had been ignored by everyone, was suddenly a shrine, a magnet for busybodies and gossipmongers.

Alan padded down the hall. He seemed resigned to living in this half-light, almost taking a certain pleasure in his home being turned into a fortress. The pale glow from the bulb that dangled on two bare wires revealed all the defects of the kitchen: cracked tiles, peeling paint, coffee stains on the wooden table. Although the shutters were closed, the windows had been left ajar in an attempt to air the room and dispel the cigarette smoke.

Alan opened a cupboard and took down a mug.

'What brings you here at this hour?'

Madenn slumped on to a chair. Her ears were ringing. She could still hear the piercing echo of shattered crockery. She ran a hand over her forehead.

'It's about Isaac ... He shouldn't go back to the headland again.'

Alan poured her a cup of coffee, then went and sat next to the window. A wisp of smoke rose from the smouldering cigarette in the ashtray; he picked it up and opened the windows a little wider. He hadn't shaved, and the greyish three-day stubble imbued his features with a certain gentleness, and a gravitas that seemed new to him.

'You were the first to encourage him.'

'There's something different about the crowd now ... It's not like it was at the start. And besides ...'

Madenn thought about the ominous dull thud that had woken her over the past few nights; the sound of a body being beaten; the vicious, rasping breath like an animal in pursuit of prey. She firmly believed that it was an omen, that it was Death announcing its presence, a premonition like those experienced by her mother, her grandfather, her great-aunt. Countless generations of Bretons had seen the signs of death before it came – the sailors' wives who saw their husbands walk into the room the very moment the sea swept them away; the clatter of the ghastly cart of Ankou* heard the day before a loved one died; the skeletal hands appearing in a doorway; the severed heads glimpsed in the shadowy corner of a room; the ghostly boats gliding across the waters of the night; the drops of blood that fell from the ceiling – Death in its many forms had appeared so often to the people of this holy, mystical land that they could no longer dismiss such portents.

Madenn laid her trembling hands on the table, her heart still beating wildly.

'You've got to tell Isaac to stop going there. I'll deal with the crowd. I'll tell them it's over, that there's nothing more to see. Things will go back to how they used to be . . .'

'You really want things to go back to how they used to be?'

Through the closed shutters came the sound of footsteps on the grass; someone was creeping around

---

* Ankou is a servant of death in Breton, Cornish and Norman French folklore.

the house. Having become accustomed to prowling strangers, Alan instinctively closed the window. In a curious way, he seemed to accept this new life: the prayers on his doorstep, the shuttered house, the dearth of sunlight, hearing his son hailed by strangers as a messiah, a visionary, a prophet. Alan heard all these names but scorned them; only one thing mattered to him now, and for that he was prepared to put up with the rest.

He stubbed out his cigarette in the ashtray.

'Can't you see that for the first time in ten years, Isaac isn't sad?'

The words were like a knife to her heart. The idea that Madenn had not noticed something so obvious, this woman who fed his son every day, who could sense his mood at a glance, who could recognize him by the way he breathed...

Madenn jumped up from the chair, her lips quivering, checking the tears that welled in her piercing blue eyes.

'Of course I can! What do you take me for?'

'Then why? Why do you want to take this away from him?'

'Because it's not safe out there any more!'

'You're the one who got him into this situation!'

'Please don't argue, the two of you.'

Standing in the doorway, Isaac looked very different. His face seemed to change with every passing day. Madenn ran over to the boy, begged him not to go back to the headland, pleaded with him to be sensible, told him the island wasn't safe any more, that a terrible danger was imminent; she could sense it, it kept her awake at night.

Isaac gently took her hands in his.

'Don't worry, it will all be over soon.'

The boy disappeared into the shadowy hallway, going off to finish what he had unwittingly started.

Up the road, the begging and pleading were of a different order: it was Michel Bourdieu, standing at the foot of the stairs, alternately folding his arms then putting his fists on his hips, unsure precisely what to do with his hands and deeply unsettled by events that were contrary to his will.

'For the last time, I don't want you taking Julia up there. It's too crowded, it'll scare her . . . Are you listening to me?'

In the hallway, indifferent to his agitation, his wife adjusted their daughter's hat. Ever since they had found Julia playing on the beach, ever since the doctor confirmed he could no longer detect a wheeze, the couple had been at cross-purposes. The incident had been so sudden, so shocking, and although his wife had completely accepted it, Michel Bourdieu was still in denial. What was required now was patience, a detailed, comprehensive check-up, a second opinion from a specialist – this was the argument he had been making since the previous day, one his wife failed to understand. When she looked at Julia, she saw a rosy glow in her cheeks, a twinkle in her eyes, and a renewed sense of wonder, as though their daughter had just come through a long period of convalescence, as though she had been given a second childhood. She was not the same little girl – the frail, delicate child who had been kept prisoner by a body attempting to suffocate her – and this was proof enough for her mother: the truth had no need for useless caveats.

'We have to go and say thank you to the Blessed Virgin, Papa.'

His daughter, forthright and radiant, forced herself to smile to reassure her father. It was a sad smile, since she was sorry for the tension she had caused in their home.

Michel Bourdieu hunkered down in front of her, suddenly tender and kind.

'Sweetheart, just because Mummy thinks you're getting better—'

'I don't *think* it, Michel. I can see it with my own eyes.'

'For God's sake! Listen to yourself . . . How can you say that she's been cured?'

Michel Bourdieu leapt to his feet with a sudden

burst of anger that surprised even him, a blind rage that stifled his tears, because that's just what he felt right now: a sob in his throat, tears in his eyes. His wife and daughter were walking out of his house; they were going back to that accursed place; they refused to heed his warnings, refused to acknowledge his suffering. Their home had been broken beyond repair; now, whenever they met, it was only to go their separate ways.

His wife looked at him with a mixture of incomprehension and pity.

'Where's your faith, Michel?'

The front door closed, and the sound of footsteps retreated. The house returned to shadows; the past days had been one long, interminable night. Michel Bourdieu strode across the living room and slumped on to the sofa. Hugo stood silently in the doorway. Darkness seemed to be closing in on his father, crushing him, turning him into a ghost doomed to haunt a place it could never leave.

The boy went over and quietly sat down on the sofa next to his father. Michel finally looked up and noticed him.

'You could go with them.'

'I'd rather stay here.'

This was the son who had lived in the shadow of his older brother, the son he had loved a little less and had sorely underestimated, for it was Hugo who stayed and sat with him all evening in the half-empty house. Michel Bourdieu looked at the boy, not knowing how to express his gratitude. All he could think was that, for those upon whom the Lord heaped troubles, He also sent comfort.

The Virgin had announced one last apparition. Over in Roscoff, in the cafe by the old port, the excitement had begun well before daybreak. Rumours had spread through the whole town, neighbours banged on each other's doors, phones rang off the hook, and now everyone had crowded into this cafe, the only place that was already open as the sun rose above the horizon and painted a golden tracery on the dark ceiling. 'Mankind can live only through faith. I promise a miracle that shall be visible to all.' These were the words brought back by the seer, as attested by multiple witnesses. The miracle was scheduled for the following day, on the island, but this time it was to take place at noon, amid the ruins of the chapel of Saint Anne. Finally, the moment had come; they would *see*, just as others before them had seen, fortunate witnesses to a divine manifestation: during the visitation of 1947, in L'Île-Bouchard before a joyful crowd, a mysterious ray of sunshine had streamed in through a stained-glass window, illuminating in the choir the precise spot of the apparition, and forcing those near the altar to shield their eyes; in 1917 in Fátima, fifty thousand people watched as the sun was transformed, turned multi-coloured, seemed to loosen itself from the firmament and hurtle towards the earth as though to crush it with its fiery weight; in 1948, at the Carmelite Monastery of Lipa in the Philippines, rose petals fell in showers at the spot where the Blessed Virgin had appeared; all around the world there had been miraculous cures, the scent of incense, haloes of light, statues of the Virgin coming to life, moving their eyes, weeping real tears; and now, a moment in history was about to take place on the island – that morning, no one in the cafe was in any doubt.

Sister Anne was only too aware of the coming moment. Standing at the foot of her bed, she folded a woollen jumper. The half-open shutters let in a muted morning light through her windows. She had not fully opened her shutters since the Bourdieu family had delivered her back here; nor had she left her room, claiming she had a migraine when Sister Delphine had come to see her. She had remained here, between these four walls, no longer looking out to sea, indifferent to this place where she felt so profoundly alien. She placed the jumper in her open suitcase. Her face was calmer, her movements more confident, despite the physical pain she felt each time she folded another piece of clothing, each time she heard the waves outside crashing against the harbour wall. In the suitcase: her crucifix and her Bible, some warm jumpers she had packed in preparation for winter on the coast. She had contacted her Mother Superior and told her she was renouncing her mission in the provinces. She'd had to resort to subterfuge, to convince without giving the true reason for her decision; she could hardly explain to her Mother Superior that she had come here believing she would see the Virgin, convinced that she, like Catherine Labouré, like Bernadette Soubirous, would be among the blessed. She had been naive, and guilty of the sin of pride, and that was why Heaven had favoured another – a boy whose heart was as simple as his body was pure. She had made a spectacle of herself in front of strangers, had flouted common sense and decency. Now all she wanted to do was leave, go back to the sanctuary of the convent, the wan light of Paris, the louring clouds that never seemed to part; she wanted to return to her canonical routine – Lauds, Vespers, Compline – helping to teach novices, taking visitors to see the chapel. Sister Anne wanted nothing more than this peaceful existence, this salutary existence, for it was a life without longing, without aspirations. She had come to realize that we sin even in our expectations.

There came a knock at the door; Sister Delphine appeared and saw the room stripped bare, the wardrobe emptied, the little suitcase almost packed. She did not ask the reason for this departure. She stood in the doorway, a little pale, her hands trembling, until Sister Anne finally noticed her. She left her packing, went over and laid a hand on her shoulder, effortlessly, as she always did, with the instinct she had for drawing people to her.

'Don't worry, Sister Agnès will be arriving in a couple of days. She's young and willing, she'll be very happy here . . .'

'The little Bourdieu girl has been cured.'

The elderly nun, her gaunt face lined with wrinkles, was still troubled by the news she had heard on the church steps, as though she had experienced nothing like it in her long life.

'A doctor went to examine her and says her asthma has completely disappeared. It's a miracle.'

Sister Delphine's bony hands gripped Sister Anne. She was quivering with emotion; having staunchly resisted the hysteria sweeping through the town, now she had finally succumbed, had finally accepted what she had never dared to believe had happened: after sixty years of prayer and service, she at last had proof.

'And tomorrow, at noon . . . *She* will appear to us all!'

She turned and left, slamming the door so hard the walls shook. In a low voice, Sister Anne repeated the words she had just heard. She did so cautiously, making sure not to twist the meaning of what she had been told: the little Bourdieu girl cured of her asthma; a doctor had examined her; it was a miracle. The church bell sounded ten o'clock. Ten times the bell tolled in Sister Anne's heart, then faded to an echo.

She turned round: on the bedside table, the little statue of the Virgin that she only ever packed at the last minute, placing it on top of everything else. There, carved into the bronze, she saw nothing but the smiling face, and suddenly there seemed to be nothing tender, nothing graceful in that smile: it was a disdainful smile, a mocking smile; the statue was taunting her for being so gullible, heaping scorn on this nun whose prayers she had never answered. Sister Anne grabbed the statue and stormed out of the apartment; outside, a warm drizzle was falling, a net of raindrops that fell without a sound. She crossed the road, heading straight for the harbour wall, for the line where land met sea, where all of this would end. The sweep of her arm as she hurled the miraculous statue – now nothing more than a tacky bronze figurine – into the waves; it sank, disappearing into murky green waters to join the submerged rocks. Meanwhile, on the distant horizon, swathed by mist, lay the ghostly amethyst coastline, the island where Sister Anne had vowed to herself never to return.

The doorbell rang. Julia set her comic book down on her lap. Over on the sofa, Hugo was asleep, a book lying on his chest – *The Hidden Reality* – which told of the potential parallel universes that he was probably dreaming about. The house was hushed: that particular silence that fell when parents were away, when the space and time of children was not interrupted. Again, the doorbell rang. Her brother didn't wake. Julia closed her comic and wandered out of the living room.

She immediately regretted opening the door. Her parents had told her over and over again not to open the door to anyone while they were gone; she could have woken her brother, told him that someone was ringing the doorbell, but despite the countless warnings, Julia had come alone, opened the door, and felt a wave of fear. Standing on the threshold was Sister

Anne – at least, it looked like her: the same blue habit, the wimple covering her hair, the Miraculous Medal around her neck. Yet there was something about her that Julia did not recognize. Perhaps it was that strange smile contorting her face, her eyes that seemed to be a slightly different shade of green, piercing like those of a snake; or perhaps it was the tense, nervous way she was holding her body, as if ready to pounce on her, because everything about Sister Anne seemed threatening. Yes, Julia felt it so keenly that she was unable to move.

'Are your parents not in?'

'They're in town . . . They had to get something . . .'

She should have lied, of course, should have said her parents were home, but the Citroën was not parked outside the gate, and Sister Anne had already realized that Julia was alone in this house. She crouched down and took the girl's hands in hers. She stroked and squeezed them, which only added to the child's unease.

'Do you want to go for a walk? Just you and me?'

The little girl looked behind her, hoping her brother might appear at the far end of the hall, but he was still asleep. In that moment, Julia was alone, her hands gripped by this woman who kindly, deviously, insisted, until she finally managed to drag the little girl from the house she was never supposed to leave.

*

The sky, spitting its fine rain. The washed-out coastline; the drab shore; the black, charred cypresses; the mottled brown earth. Everywhere seemed grey, the mist and drizzle; everything looked as though it were dying. The child had no choice now – she was tethered to Sister Anne, who was hauling her faster and faster up the steep escarpment towards the headland. She panted for breath, slipped on the muddy path, stumbled over branches, unable to cry out, like those nightmares in which she longed to scream but could not.

The shrubs grew sparser here and the path widened out: the two were now moving across the heights, traversing the vast, vertiginous abyss where the sea kissed the sky, a boundless grey world.

On they ran, Sister Anne leading the way, never letting go of the child's hand, striding blindly through the rain. The Heavens she had come to defy, this child she was determined to prove wrong, it was a fever, an overwhelming, uncontrollable obsession, a madness Sister Anne only half glimpsed; it was evil, and she too was capable of evil.

'No!'

A terrifying, heart-rending cry petrified Sister Anne; they were a few steps from the cliff edge that plunged down to rocks like giant gravestones. This whole island was a cemetery. Sailors lost at sea, bodies washed up on the shore, those treacherous rocks – the curse of every boat – that were visible only at the last moment, a last memory before death.

Sister Anne felt something squirming – the little girl was wriggling her hand free, wresting herself from her rain-wet fingers. Sister Anne turned and saw that she had sinned. She had not wanted to. It was grief that had brought her to this place, she who had never hurt a soul in all her life. She looked into the innocent face distorted by pain as the girl struggled to catch her breath, wheezing every time she inhaled, the wheezing that everyone said had been cured.

Sister Anne clapped her hands over her mouth in horror, as the girl turned and ran back to her house through the driving rain.

The skylight was half open, allowing in a breath of damp, salty air. Lying under the duvet with the photo of his mother on his chest, Isaac smelled the scent of the sea. From time to time, he closed his eyes but could not seem to sleep. Time dragged slowly once night had fallen, when he was forced to wait. *Mankind can live only through faith. I promise a miracle that shall be visible to all. After that, you will not see me again.* This would be the last visit; the wonder of the past days, of everything he had experienced so far. From now on, there would be no absence: everywhere, at every moment, even in emptiness, even in silence, he would have this certainty. Nor would there be loneliness; this was something he might have learned much later, or never learned at all, but he had been lucky.

At the end of the road, outside the Bourdieu house,

the Citroën's engine revved in the darkness. Isaac listened as it sped along the dirt track and up the hill. The sound faded. He thought about Hugo, wondered whether he would be there tomorrow among the ruins where, a few days earlier, they had been pulled apart and told never to see each other again. He thought of Hugo's gentle face, the friendship he offered without expecting anything in return. Until this moment, he had not realized that he felt the same way.

The first rays of dawn sent shadows scurrying across the empty room, and it was as though the end had already begun.

That morning, the island looked almost as it did on the last Sunday of July, when pilgrims, islanders and children processed along this very road – the women wearing white lace mantillas and traditional dress; the men, black wide-brimmed hats and embroidered waistcoats over white linen shirts – all heading towards the ruined chapel on the east of the island. This was the Pardon of Saint Anne, a pilgrimage that, like thousands of others across Brittany, took place when the fine weather returned: the abundant light of summer; the stirring music of the bombardes* and the Breton bagpipes; the fluttering pennants of the saints; the statue of Saint Anne held aloft above the

---

* A Breton folk instrument like a shawm or oboe.

crowd; the fervent, festive atmosphere that continued into the ruins of the old chapel where the priest performed the Pardon, drawing from those fallen stones the vibrations of an earlier age.

This was almost like the Pardon of Saint Anne – the crowd of people moving along the path, the chapel already filled to capacity – but today there were no bagpipes, no bombardes, no pennants, no traditional dress, not even a square of white lace or a black hat; no, this was a silent procession of people dressed in winter coats, braving the stiff westerly wind, walking across the island in the gloomy light. In the ancient chapel, there were no psalms or hymns, only anxious muttered conversations as people noted that time was passing and Isaac had still not arrived.

'Where on earth is the lad?'

'He's making us wait . . .'

'I told you, he's been lying all this time!'

'Shh!'

'Calm down. It's not noon yet.'

'We've swallowed his story hook, line and sinker; we've only got ourselves to blame.'

In the distance, the peeling facade of Alan's house. They could imagine the boy hiding behind the closed shutters, peering through the crack at the gullible crowd gathered in these Roman ruins simply because he had told them to. In and around the chapel there were whispers as people reacted to the slightest sound, the merest change in the light, though they did not seem to know what they were waiting for. Noon had struck and still nothing was happening; there was no break in the clouds, no halo of light. Nothing but emptiness. The cold seeped into the marrow of their bones. Still the boy did not appear. The west wind whistled through the arches and the gable windows, mocking the crowd gathered in this venerable ruin.

Suddenly from the top of the hill came a roar – a Citroën 2CV was hurtling down the road. Here was someone they had not expected to see; in fact, since the incident on the headland, people had stopped thinking about Michel Bourdieu. The prospect of a miracle had made them forget everything else and, for his part, Michel had kept a low profile, staying away from church and avoiding the crowd that had unjustly condemned him. They raced towards the car, forcing it to stop in the middle of the road.

'Michel, it's past noon . . .'

'And – surprise, surprise – Isaac isn't here!'

'He's been making fools of us from the start.'

The crowd, like the tide, ebbed and flowed, forgetting that only a few days earlier they had humiliated this man. Now they were pressing against his car window; inside Michel Bourdieu and his son sat, both looking solemn, exhausted after a long and gruelling night. Calling the ambulance, the drive to Morlaix, the antiseptic air of the emergency room.

Those clustered around the car did not seem to notice how shattered they were.

'Maybe we should go and knock on Alan's door?'

'The only reason the miracle hasn't happened is because the lad's not here . . .'

The miracle. Michel Bourdieu had forgotten what had been promised on this island. A shiver ran down the back of his neck, the cold caress of death. His daughter, the oxygen mask, her eyes closed as she lay in the hospital bed. It had begun in the evening with a fever. At first Julia had said nothing, had simply gone to bed early, but as the evening wore on, her temperature had soared, her breathing becoming so laboured she could not even tell her parents that Sister Anne had forced her to run all the way up to the headland. By the middle of the night, the child had lost consciousness. Michel Bourdieu's knuckles were white as he gripped the steering wheel.

'My daughter was rushed to hospital last night. There never was any "cure". But you carry on waiting for this miracle of yours.'

Then he started the engine and sped off back to his house, leaving those who had approached him behind. The news quickly filtered through the rest of the crowd in the old chapel. At first, there was a sense of shock, since all of the islanders had believed that the little Bourdieu girl had been miraculously cured – her asthma had disappeared, even the doctor had been categorical. Then, gradually, there came a visceral rumbling, like the roar of lava surging from the bowels of the earth as the ground gave way; like a wave hurtling towards the rocks; like the tremulous ear-splitting seconds that herald an explosion.

'It's all the fault of that lad, Isaac!'

Piety prevails only as long as it is expedient. The meek, reverent congregation of the faithful suddenly erupted with obscenities, profaning the sacred ruins, abjuring the very thing they had come there to find. Righteous anger is more intoxicating than prayers and hymns, than twilight and the full moon. The crowd scattered, the black mass swarming across the dunes to ransack the shrine on the headland, to lay siege to Alan's house; from everywhere came insults, fists banging on doors and shutters, tossed rocks and flower pots – anything that was to hand was hurled against this accursed house.

In the distance, Hugo stood at the far end of the road and surveyed the mayhem, rooted to the spot, feeling the same knot in the pit of his stomach.

The remains of the day slipped away from the coast; that singular moment when the light faded and the landscape became shrouded in a watery dark blue. A moment of calm, like every other evening. The last calls of the seagulls and the rising tide that lapped against the shore were immutable; all earthly things adhered to the same order, and all of mankind's troubles stemmed from flouting it.

Sister Anne walked on, hoisting up her habit with one hand as she climbed from rock to rock; from time to time, her foot slipped and she would stop, her heart pounding, and watch as the sea rose and engulfed the reefs. Behind her, the coastline was deserted. The crowd had finally dispersed, sapped of its fury and a little stunned, like a drunk person sobering up and realizing the consequences of their actions. All around, the aftermath of this riot was plain to see: the flayed exterior of Alan's house, its shutters broken, its windows shattered; the shrine on the headland laid to waste; the ground strewn with rosaries, broken vases, trampled flowers; the smashed statue of the Virgin.

The rocky outcrop, once a focus of prayer, was now a place of despair. At a distance, Sister Anne had waited for the shadowy figure to leave before sliding down the slope to reach the first rock. She had intended to depart the day before, the moment she had turned to Julia and heard her panting, wheezing breath. Like the rest of the crowd, she knew that the little girl was now in hospital. She moved on, clambering from rock to rock, intent only on reaching the boundary between the land and the water.

Only a single step now separated her from the sea. Beneath her feet, the waves broke, grabbing at her ankles like icy fingers come to drag her to the depths. She hunkered on the last rock; in the distance she could see the dark outline of Roscoff, the bell tower soaring above the roofs of the houses. The sky was a deep blue, almost purple, underscored by a golden streak that heralded the last moments of day. The distinctive way light fell over this peninsula was unlike anything Sister Anne had ever seen in Paris; it was truth, it was the wellspring, it was all the things mankind strived for through prayer and through science, and she had finally found it, here on this rocky stretch of coast, when it was too late.

She took a breath and bent over the black waters.

'Sister.'

At first she was unsure whether the voice had come from within her, whether her mind was already foundering, because for some time now she had heard only the sea, a swelling, disconcerting melody that threatened to engulf her.

'Sister Anne.'

She turned round, a little panicked, and at first saw nothing but a hand extended towards her. She who had been careful to wait until she was completely alone. She who had wanted to depart with no chance of intercession, had wanted the sea to take her body and never spit it out. She had not noticed that the skylight of the house the angry crowd had tried to breach was open; that, standing on his bed, Isaac was watching her: a navy-blue habit moving across the dark and distant rocks, sometimes stumbling, sometimes slipping, heading towards the sea.

When the silence had finally returned, Isaac had quietly opened his skylight to check that the crowd had dispersed. He had not intended to dupe them earlier. He had been preparing to go down to the ruined church, one hand on the handle of the front door, when he had heard the drone of an engine at the top of the hill, seen the Citroën hurtling down the road and screech to a halt. In the deafening roar of the riot that ensued, he had remained with his father, huddled on the stairs, wondering which of the windows would shatter first.

'Come, Sister.'

This voice, calling to her, appealing to her to come back, and behind her the whisper of the sea, also calling to her. Sister Anne froze. She stood motionless on the rock, suddenly aware of the rough, slippery surface beneath her feet, of her precarious balance – her next act would be the last. Suddenly she flinched as a wave crashed against the rock, and she felt the cold embrace of the icy water. She grabbed the waiting hand – instinct reacting more swiftly than reason – and everything came together in that touch, that first sense of rediscovered warmth, reconnecting her with the world. She allowed herself to be led away, gazing down at the black rocks, no longer afraid of falling, watching the waves claw at her ankles, enraged that she had abandoned her plan. She gripped the hand, clung to this boy who, against all expectations, beyond all prayer, had come to find her; no moment would ever rival the gratitude she felt.

A steep slope, then the long grass: she had come back, could feel the ground beneath her feet, this earth to which men belonged. In the distance lay the petrol-blue sea, a vast abyss between two coastlines. The rock on which she had stood a moment earlier was gone – she scoured the reef, but it was nowhere to be seen; it had drowned without her. She was shivering all over, but not from the cold so much as from the knowledge that she had been down there, standing on the rock that was now submerged: a few more seconds and everything might have been different.

Isaac stared at her anxiously, wanting to make sure Sister Anne wouldn't turn back towards the sea. This face that she had bitterly hated, now shining in the half-light, was filled with a gentleness that she had refused to see. She could still feel his hand clasping hers; its imprint would always be with her, there in the hollow of her hand, a gift from this stony coastline. As if this land had finally deigned to grant her something.

'You should go – the last launch to the mainland leaves in twenty minutes. I've got to get back; my father thinks I'm up in my bedroom.'

The boy vanished into the darkness as though he had never been there, as though Sister Anne had only dreamed that he had come to find her, there in that rocky graveyard. She walked away, a little dazed, heading up the dirt track towards the road. The crashing waves behind drowned out all other sound, so she did not hear the dull thud of a body falling to the ground. She hurried back to the harbour, her skirts gathered up, running beneath the pale glow of the streetlamps; far below, heavy blows rained down on the face she had just left, and a rasping, animal breath echoed through the darkness.

Michel Bourdieu held his hands under the tap, the icy water streaming over his grazed and aching knuckles. Slowly, he rubbed his hands together, staring straight ahead. His skin had swollen. The pale red water trickled away. He tried to open his clenched fists but failed; the pain in his knuckles was too intense. A spatter of crimson droplets: a stark contrast to the white porcelain of the sink. Out in the hallway, the packed suitcase had stood since the early evening; some clothes for Julia and for his wife, who had stayed at the hospital with their daughter. He would take the case to them tomorrow morning. Seeing them both again, hugging his wife, kissing his daughter's forehead – the very thought made his heart swell with a profound happiness: as he stood by the sink, Michel Bourdieu was smiling, even though there was dried blood stuck to his skin and his hands were clenched into fists he could not open, as though he were still punching, as though he could still feel death seeping into Isaac's body.

It was worse than anything Hugo could have imagined. His premonition, the terrible knot he had felt in the pit of his stomach for days, was nothing compared to what he was feeling now: this terrible wave of nausea as he raced down the road, running through the darkness as though it were day. He had known from the moment he saw his father standing in the kitchen – the crimson hands, the blood no amount of water could wash away – he had known but he had to go and see for himself, to prove that his foreboding had been wrong, to allow himself a few more seconds of disbelief.

There, by the side of the road in the long grass, an arm extended, a shock of curly hair, the viscous blood; a face unrecognizable, destroyed by blows.

Ethereal rifts appeared above the coastline as the clouds parted and the waning moon shone through, its bright glow spilling over everything: the silvery gleam of the rocks; the shimmer of the sea, the translucent waves; the white sand of the shore, the tall grasses, the bands of seaweed; the whole island bathed in the same blue radiance.

Hugo looked up into the broken sky, where scudding gossamer clouds traced a nebulous halo around the moon. Leaving the shattered body at his feet, he followed the light – the moon his only landmark, the only warmth in this cold night. Beneath his feet, the slope fell sharply towards the shore with its damp cold sand. Around him, whispers, rustlings, voices everywhere. This was unlike the silence he had known, or perhaps he had been mistaken, had misconstrued the absence of sound to mean the absence of other lives; that must be it, because things seemed to begin only when everything else fell silent. Suddenly, he felt water lapping at his ankles, so cold it was almost painful. He had never before set foot in the sea, never dived into a swimming pool, his fear of the water even greater than his fear of his father. He sank into the shifting ground, gazing up at the sky, waiting for the moment when his feet could not touch the bottom, waiting for the first wave.

The rainstorm lashing the house. Heavy drops pounding the tiles on the roof, suffocating the silent house. In the bedroom, Sister Anne stands motionless, looking at the little girl who is looking back at her. She does not speak, so astonished is she that she can finally be seen, that the child is looking at her for the first time.

A creak at the bottom of the stairs – he is coming. The little girl can hear it too, but she is not worried: in her eyes there is a confidence that is as moving as it is unexpected. Sister Anne walks towards the door, groping in the darkness, and finally she can feel an unfamiliar object; she looks down to see what she has found: a lock. Beneath the door handle, there is a lock. Footsteps outside; he is already on the landing, coming towards the bedroom. Sister Anne turns the key. Beneath her fingers, all the things she had given up hoping for: the click of the lock, the deadbolt firmly anchored in the wall. On the other side, her father realizes what has happened and slams his weight against the door. Sister Anne takes a step back, imagines the raised fist pounding, trying to force the door open. The hammering grows louder: black fury. The door shudders, then suddenly everything stops.

The footsteps retreat across the landing, go back down the stairs. Soon all she can hear is the rain, the torrential rain cleansing the world outside.

Sister Anne turns; on the bed, the little girl has disappeared.

Sister Delphine gently shook her shoulders, speaking in a low voice, trying to wake her without startling her.

'Sister Anne . . .'

She had heard footsteps pacing inside the room, and had come and knocked on the door, but there was no answer. Sister Delphine had opened the door to find Sister Anne standing there in her nightgown, her green eyes wide, frozen, staring at some other world.

She called her name again, and finally Sister Anne came back to herself. She glanced around, confused, unable to understand how she had left her childhood bedroom. The crucifix over the door, the empty wardrobe, the suitcase on the floor: today was the day she would be leaving, Sister Anne remembered now.

'Are you all right?'

Sister Delphine was holding her arms, concerned and perhaps a little troubled, as though she had unwittingly uncovered one of the secrets that gave Sister Anne her mystique.

Sister Anne took the older nun's hands: she smiled shyly, her lips trembling, not yet daring to acknowledge the moment.

'I'm much better now, Sister.'

Sister Delphine was pouring coffee when someone knocked at the door. She set down the cafetiere and went to open it. Sitting at the table, Sister Anne was buttering bread. She had pinned a blue wimple over her hair and hung the Miraculous Medal around her neck. Earlier, while she was getting dressed, it felt as though she were doing these things for the first time; adjusting her white collar, dusting down her blue skirts in front of the mirror – discovering herself in the clothes of a nun. This morning, everything had seemed new.

She heard the front door open, and the sound of voices, but paid them little heed. She thought about her journey home. The bus to Morlaix, the afternoon train. She had decided to drop by the hospital, to visit Julia's bedside, to confess, to tell Julia's mother what had happened, how she had forced her daughter to run up that hill. She was not seeking forgiveness; she simply wanted to tell her not to blame Heaven: misfortune never came from above.

'Sister Anne.'

In the doorway, Father Erwann was grave. He looked suddenly old, all the youthful exuberance drained from his round, beardless face. Behind him, Sister Delphine waved a gnarled hand and leaned on a chair for support.

'There is no easy way to say this . . . Isaac was found dead this morning. It was Madenn who found the body. She screamed herself hoarse . . . she lost her voice completely.'

Sister Anne realized she was still holding the butter knife. She set it down on the plate. The kitchen suddenly felt stifling. She got up and went to the window overlooking the port. The air was utterly still. Not a breath of wind brushed her cheek. She leaned out: high above, a few static clouds were pinned to the sky. No swooping gulls, no cackling laughter. The sea was perfectly tranquil; not a ripple, no movement anywhere. Sister Anne would have preferred a deluge, a roar of thunder, a raging sea, booming waves – deafening fury rather than this muted, frozen coastline.

From nowhere, a cat appeared on the road then scampered off at speed. In the distance, she intuited the first cries. Sister Anne gripped the window frame, closed her eyes, and from that moment, heard nothing more of what happened upon this coast.

Fourteen years later

'My brother's body was recovered. The sea brought him back after the earthquake, as though it knew he did not belong in the water. I remember thanking the sea for returning him to us. It's ridiculous, talking to something that can't answer back. I suppose you'd say it was the very definition of prayer. We buried him in Roscoff. At first, my mother was reluctant: after all, this coast had taken her son from her – why should she leave him here? Then she remembered all those nights when Hugo went out to gaze at the stars. My brother never found a better place to study the constellations than Brittany ... And my mother wanted him to be able to see them still. The sky over the coast is unique. You feel as though *it* is gazing at *you*, rather than the other way round. You know what I mean? I'm sorry, this all sounds a little vague. There were so many funerals that day . . . I was overwhelmed by the crowd. People had come from all over the peninsula to honour those the sea had taken. Almost every house on the island had been affected by the tsunami. Ours was reduced to rubble. They say there's never been anything like it there. My father's body was never found; even now, he is officially considered still missing.'

A gentle breeze wafted in through the window, disturbing the dust on the shelves. The library was filled with old calf-bound books, hagiographies, even Latin editions of the New Testament. Time and sunlight had bleached some of the covers, and no one dared touch them for fear the pages would crumble beneath their fingers.

The Mother Superior folded her hands on the desk. She had listened to this story intently, as it shed more light on the events that had so profoundly affected the Mother House fourteen years earlier.

'And Isaac?'

'He was never found either.'

The young woman opposite sat bolt upright on the chair, gripping her bag, stoically attempting to keep these memories at bay.

The Mother Superior sighed and turned to the window.

'You'll find her in the garden.'

From a distance, she saw her at the bend in the path, on her knees, digging the soil around the rose bushes. Her greying hair was braided into a long plait that fell to the small of her back, and there was an apron tied over her fawn dress. She no longer looked like a Daughter of Charity, yet it was unmistakably her; the same graceful profile, the slender figure, now so different from the other nuns in the convent.

Engrossed as she was in the roses, it took a moment before Sister Anne noticed the young woman standing next to her. She looked up with a warm smile.

'Are you a postulant? Are you looking for the Mother Superior's office?'

'I'm Julia. Julia Bourdieu.'

A warm breeze blew through the cloisters. On the trees, the leaves trembled and whispered. Sparrows hopped along the branches, chirping and pecking.

Sister Anne turned back to her roses, not daring to look at the young woman she now recognized. She had not seen Julia since that day. The ghostly coast. The landscape shrouded in drizzle. Nothing but boundless grey, and the void yawning so very close to her. And the little girl with the wet hair, whose face had been racked by anxiety and fear, now stood before her, all grown up, a living memory here in the convent, come to find her conscience.

'I won't take up too much of your time, Sister Anne.'
'I'm known as Alice now.'

A little unsteadily, she got to her feet and gestured to a nearby bench. The gardens were bustling with spring; the gentle light, the budding flowers, the perfumes forgotten by winter. They sat side by side, Julia clutching her bag, sitting straight and rigid; this stiffness was the only thing that helped her keep her feelings in check.

'I'll keep it short. I don't like to dwell on the past. I don't know exactly why you tried to take me to the headland that day . . . You weren't yourself, I could tell that. It was as though you wanted to hurt me. But . . . in the end, what you did saved me: it was because of you that I wasn't on the island the day the earthquake hit.'

As though someone had voiced all her regrets aloud, Sister Anne turned, her eyes filled with fear. She had not gone to the hospital in the end. She had abandoned the idea of visiting Julia's bedside, of confessing to her mother that she was to blame for the girl's asthma attack. She had fled the coastline as it began to shake, renounced her nun's habit – but she had remained here, cleaning and washing within the convent. As a simple laywoman, she was unlike the others – she no longer rose for Lauds, she had turned away from all intense emotion, had carried on her life without seeking ecstasy, and it had been for the best: she could only find rest in indifference.

She leaned forward, brushing the dirt from her hands.

'That terrible catastrophe ... It was divine justice ... Heaven restoring order ...'

'There had been several quakes in the area during that week. It happened because it happened. That's all there is to it.'

Two nuns appeared at the far end of the path. In the august convent that had stood here for three hundred years, it was almost surprising not to see sisters coiffed with the old-fashioned white cornettes, seeming to float in their ample black habits, with rosary beads hanging from their waists. The nuns greeted the two women with a smile; their faces were gentle, ageless, spared the ravages of time by a life of prayer and service. They disappeared around the corner.

Julia got up from the bench and slung her bag over her shoulder.

'What I've come to say is that the only twist of fate in this story is the one I owe to you. I ended up in hospital, and that was what saved my mother's life and mine.'

Julia had not changed: she still had that great mane of raven hair, the sparkling eyes; still noticed everything, yet rarely said a word; and this new stiffness about her body merely masked its counterpart, a fieriness that had inhabited Julia since childhood and which Sister Anne could still sense, just beneath the skin.

'What about your asthma, Julia?'

Julia had almost forgotten that she had ever had asthma. The last attack was the one she had just mentioned. After that, she had discovered freedom, movement, breathing; she had gone back to live in the city, untroubled by the pollution, indifferent to nights spent surrounded by cigarette smoke. As she had grown up, she had thought less and less about that other life; sometimes she almost doubted she had experienced it at all.

'No doctor has ever been able to explain it.'

The light shifted, the clouds parted, and a burst of sunlight illuminated the cloister. And with it came a memory: fourteen years ago on a sunny winter's day, walking the hills and dales of the island, her parents happy and smiling as they showed the nun the sights. Julia remembered. The dazzling brightness of the shore. The winding paths along the coast. Everywhere you looked, an immensity of blue that made you dizzy with happiness. And Sister Anne, sitting with her back to the sun, shrouded in a halo, telling her about the miracles of the Blessed Virgin. The former nun was older now as she sat there on the bench, perhaps a little sadder, though her eyes had a gentleness that remained unchanged.

Julia awkwardly adjusted the shoulder strap of her bag.

'It was luck. That's all there is to it.'

She turned on her heel, fleeing the memory that had found her out. Sister Anne listened to the footsteps on the gravel. Slowly, she ran a finger under her collar and touched the Miraculous Medal, which was still warm. She held it as she sat on the bench.

Above the rooftops, the cackle of gulls announced to Paris that twilight was approaching. A soft wind moved through the convent gardens, warm, tinged with salt and the pungent smell of seaweed. Sister Anne held the medal tightly and looked around at the gardens. Perhaps, finally, she had found somewhere there would always be a place for her.

The Mad Women's Ball, Victoria Mas's debut novel, won several prizes in France (including the Prix Stanislas and the Prix Renaudot des Lycéens) and was the bestselling debut of the year. It has been translated into twenty-three languages and been made into an Amazon Prime Video Original Film starring Mélanie Laurent and Lou de Laâge. Victoria has worked in film in the United States, where she lived for eight years. She graduated from the Sorbonne in Contemporary Literature. She now lives in Paris.

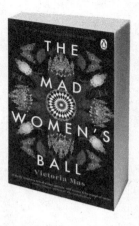

The Salpêtrière asylum, 1885. All of Paris is in thrall to Doctor Charcot and his displays of hypnotism on women who have been deemed mad or hysterical. But the truth is more complicated – these women are often simply inconvenient, unwanted wives or strong-willed daughters. Once a year, a grand event is held – the Mad Women's Ball. For the Parisian elite, it is the highlight of the social season; for the women themselves, it is a rare moment of hope.

Geneviève is a senior nurse who has placed her faith in Doctor Charcot and his new science. But everything changes when she meets Eugénie, the daughter of a bourgeois family. For Eugénie has a secret and she needs Geneviève's help. Their fates will collide on the night of the Mad Women's Ball . . .

Now an Amazon Prime film starring Mélanie Laurent

'Utterly captivating'
Miranda Dickinson

'Richly immersive'
Shelley Harris

'Enter the dance of this little masterpiece and
let yourself be dazzled'
The Parisian